Loyal to the Game 2

Lock Down Publications & Ca$h Presents
Loyal to the Game 2

.

Loyal to the Game 2

Lock Down Publications
P.O. Box 1482
Pine Lake, Ga 30072-1482

Visit our website at **www.lockdownpublica-tions.com**

Copyright 2017 Loyal to the Game 2

All rights reserved. No part of this book may be reproduced in any form or by electronic or mechanical means, including information storage and retrieval systems without permission in writing from the publisher, except by a reviewer who may quote brief passages in review.

First Edition July 2017
Printed in the United States of America
This is a work of fiction. Names, characters, places, and incidents either are products of the author's imagination or are used fictitiously. Any similarity to actual events or locales or persons, living or dead, is entirely coincidental.

Cover design and layout by: Dynasty's Cover Me
Book interior design by: Shawn Walker
Edited by: Lauren Burton

3

Stay Connected with Us!

Text **LOCKDOWN** to 22828 to stay up-to-date
with new releases, sneak peaks, contests and more…

Thank you!

Submission Guideline.

Submit the first three chapters of your completed manuscript to ldpsubmissions@gmail.com, subject line: Your book's title. The manuscript must be in a .doc file and sent as an attachment. Document should be in Times New Roman, double spaced and in size 12 font. Also, provide your synopsis and full contact information. If sending multiple submissions, they must each be in a separate email.

Have a story but no way to send it electronically? You can still submit to LDP/Ca$h Presents. Send in the first three chapters, written or typed, of your completed manuscript to:

LDP: Submissions Dept
Po Box 1482
Pine Lake, Ga 30072

DO NOT send original manuscript. Must be a duplicate.

Provide your synopsis and a cover letter containing your full contact information.

Thanks for considering LDP and Ca$h Presents.

T.J. & Jelissa

Chapter 1

Tiny

I couldn't believe that bitch grabbed me by my braids and flung me against the wall with them. I crashed against the wall with a loud thud, and she jumped right on top of me and started punching me in the nose until I felt blood running down my cheeks. I yelled out in pain.

"Give me the money, you bitch, or I'm gonna kill you!" She grabbed the knife off the floor and held it up in the air. I imagined she was getting ready to slam it into my chest until we both heard a loud knocking on the door.

I knew it was my nosey-ass neighbor as soon as I heard her screaming we were making too much noise, but Lisa didn't, and as soon as she looked over toward the door, I used the distraction to lift up and head-butt the shit out of her with my forehead. She fell off me, dazed, with her nose bleeding.

I slid from under her and she tried her best to get ahold of me again by grabbing the collar of my shirt, but I jerked away with this crazy bitch right on my heels in hot pursuit.

I ain't gon' even lie, after I saw all of that blood on her face and my own, and factored in I was feeling woozy and this girl was still trying to kill me, I got a little scared and tried my best to get away from her. So, while she chased close behind me, I got to knocking over shit trying to slow her down. I guess she must have tripped over one of the chairs with the knife in her hand because I heard a loud scream, and when I looked back she was lying face down, shaking.

At first, I thought she was trying to fool me, but then I saw the blood pooling around her and knew she wasn't. I ran over to her and flipped her over, and that's when I saw the knife embedded deep within her.

Before I could even think about it, I pulled the knife out, and that's when Mrs. Applebaum saw me holding the murder weapon.

And that's what they convicted me on.

This was the first visit I had ever had with my daughter in the 16 years she had been alive, and I was trying my best to explain to her why the state of Illinois had kept her away from me.

So many crazy things had taken place after I pulled that knife out of Lisa. First of all, I didn't know that pulling the knife out of her stomach would cause her to bleed out.

Secondly, after I pulled the knife out of her, Chris was already on his way upstairs. When he got to my apartment, he saw all of the blood and the girl lying on the floor, but that did not stop him from snatching me up by my hair and making me give him his money. He took his cash and bolted, but not before telling me our business was not concluded because I owed him for endangering his safety. Can you imagine that shit? That nigga had my baby daddy locked in a basement beaten half to death and he was talking about me endangering his safety? That nigga had some nerve.

They beat Avery, my baby's father, so bad he wound up paralyzed from the waist down. They also disfigured his face. I had not heard from him since that day, but word got back to me from my daughter that he was all fucked up, and I had gotten a few pictures of him as well.

They did me real bad. They gave me 40 years in prison, and I couldn't believe the display the pastor and his wife put on at my sentencing. They brought the whole congregation. Even my parents took the stand against me and painted me out to be this devilish person. By the time they were finished talking, even I felt like I should have never been let back out into society. It seemed like everybody was against me, and because I didn't have anybody to stand in my corner, they threw the book at me and it hit me in the forehead.

I gave birth to my daughter, Alexis, in Dwight Correctional Institution. She came out healthy and smiling, and before I could get used to her being in my arms they stripped her away from me and re-shackled my feet to the bed. I cried all night long and prayed God would bring my daughter back to me or overturn my sentence.

It took me 16 years to get the chance to meet with my daughter face-to-face. It felt real awkward because our case manager sat in the chair to the right of her, so I couldn't say all the things I wanted to say and I had to act like I was holier than thou. She had just asked me to explain to her what had happened and I'd given her the short version. I left out the details because my appeal was still in the works and I knew our case manager would report any new revelations directly to the courts, so I had to play things real safe.

I looked across the table at my baby and I could not believe how beautiful she was. She was also so damn chocolate, which was odd because I was yellow as hell. But then again, her father was pretty black himself, so maybe that's where she got all that melanin in her skin from. My baby, though only 16, was already built like a young woman, and that scared me because I knew how it was in those streets for a young girl built like her.

The case manager had brought her up to see me because Alexis had run away from the foster home four times now, and she refused to listen to anyone. They said she had a bad temper and at the drop of a hat she would lash out and attack any kid – or grown up, it didn't really matter.

They figured it was time she and I met so I could talk some sense into her, so I thought I would start by answering her questions. That way we could get to know each other.

Although I had written her numerous letters, I was unsure if she got them. Or if she got them, I was still unsure if she'd actually read them.

"So then, Mom, when are you coming home? Or do you have to be here forever?" she asked, and every time she spoke a word her dimples would pop up on her cheeks. I could not believe how pretty my baby was.

I took a deep breath and fidgeted in my seat. "No, baby, I don't have to be here for the rest of my life. I have been doing good, and if I continue on this path, I can be home in less than three years. Won't that be amazing?" I asked with a ray of hope in my heart.

She shrugged her shoulders. "To be honest, I been away from you for so long it's like I don't even have a mother, and it's like I'm so used to being alone out there I don't know how it would feel if you were home. And speaking of home, I don't even know what it's like to have one. I've been in this foster home my whole life, and they treat us like dirt there."

Our case manager flipped her red hair over her shoulder and sighed loudly. "Come on now, Alexis, it isn't that bad."

I saw Alexis frown and she rolled her eyes. "Excuse you, but I'm talking to my mother right now. This has nothing to do with you. Your only job is to bring me here so I can see her. You're supposed to sit there and shut up, just like I have to do when you guys have meetings about me and I have to sit and listen to you go on and on like I'm not even there, and then when I try to say something, you tell me to sit and be quiet like my opinion doesn't matter. So, now why don't you shut up and be quiet while I talk to the woman you people have kept me away from my whole life?" She continued to glare at the woman as if challenging her.

The case manager crossed her arms across her flat chest and put her head down. "Very well, then. Go ahead. I won't say another word."

I smiled my sympathies. "Thank you, I appreciate that," I said.

The visiting room was starting to fill up. Families were coming in with their children and babies were starting to cry while toddlers ran around chasing one another. I saw one li'l boy with his finger so far up his nose he had to close his eyes 'cause I think he was hurting his self. He pulled down a big, green booger and started chasing his sister with it. She screamed at the top of her lungs, and I almost busted up laughing when he caught her and wiped it in her hair. She ran straight up to her mother, who looked as if she had enough, and tried to show her. The woman took out some tissue and tended to the little girl, whose face was so red it looked like she was turning into a strawberry. Her brother danced around the visiting room and worked on pulling down a new booger, but this one he ate.

"Anyway, Momma, like I was saying, I hate it at that place, and I can't wait until you come home," Alexis said, lowering her head.

"Baby, don't worry. I am doing all I can to get there as soon as I can. All I need for you to do is keep going to school so you can graduate and get into college."

"Oh, yes, that is definitely something you two need to talk about, because Alexis has been skipping school lately. Isn't that right, darling?"

Alexis stood up. "Say, bitch, you starting to piss me off. Now, I thought you was gon' keep your mouth closed for the rest of this visit. What happened to that?" she asked, balling up her fists.

The case manager looked worried. She looked as if she wanted to stand up, but decided against it, probably thinking she would look as if she were challenging Alexis, which it was clear she wasn't. She looked around the visiting room to see how close the guards were.

They were paying more attention to the children in the middle of the floor playing Smack Down. One little fat boy clotheslined a skinnier kid and then sat on him while another fat boy counted to three. The skinny kid on the bottom couldn't do nothing but wiggle his feet while his sister, who had to be less than three, walked up to the fat boy seated on her brother and bit him so hard he screamed at the top of his lungs and then shot up and ran. She fell on her Pampers and put her pacifier back into her mouth.

"Well, I'm sorry, Alexis, but we have to address the issues, and if I remain silent we won't get to them. Now, it's imperative you make a behavioral change or else you may wind up in a place like this. Do you want to be that kind of a failure?" she asked, lowering her glasses on her nose.

Now I was starting to get a little bit offended. What the fuck did she mean, 'that kind of a failure?' I felt like this bitch was taking a shot at me, and I almost flipped out and said something, but my daughter beat me to the punch.

"My momma ain't no failure, so you better watch your mouth. And just 'cause I missed a few days of school don't mean they are going to charge me with murder. I have never gotten less than a 3.5, so where is the problem? I do plenty extra credit, and I am ahead in all of my classes. What more do you want from me? It's better I don't show than show up and cut a bitch, because them girls at my school think they are better than me, and they're not. I am not afraid of them or nobody else, but I am tired of them picking on me. So, some days I refuse to go to school, but the day prior I make sure I get all of my assignments for the following day so I am not missing out on anything. You need to stop trying to clown me in front of my mother, or I'm gon' kick yo' ass, bitch, and I'm

12

not playing."

She was getting ready to walk up on the woman when I stood up, blocking her path, and it was good I did because that white lady was getting ready to run to the guards. That would have gotten me sent to segregation and her taken off of my visiting list, and that would have broken my heart. I was just getting to know her as a young woman. I didn't know why her temper was so bad, but clearly, she had some things going on deep inside of her. "Okay Alexis, baby, please calm down. I don't want them to take you off of my visiting list. I need to start to see you as much as possible."

She looked as if she still wanted to attack the woman, but then all of a sudden, she sat down and nodded. "I'm sorry, Mom. I'm just tired of these people, that's all. I won't flip out again, though. At least I promise I'll try."

"That's good enough for me." I turned to the case manager. "Please let us enjoy these final minutes together. Her and I will figure these things out in time. You have to realize this is my first time seeing her in person. I'm not going to jump down her throat to try and assert my dominance. This is my baby, and I have literally been sick without her. Can you understand that?"

She nodded, then did the sign she was locking her lips and throwing away the key. Alexis frowned and then shook her head in irritation.

"Baby, do you read my letters when I send them to you?" I asked her while looking into her brown eyes.

She lowered her head. "Yeah, Mom. I mean, I try to, but sometimes they make me so sad. I try to forget about you at times because it makes things easier, but then when a letter from you shows up, it brings me right back to my reality, which is that I don't have a mother right now." A tear dropped from her eye and sailed down her cheek. She wiped it away and turned her head.

I reached across the small table and put my hand onto her thigh. "Baby, is that how you feel? Do you honestly consider me dead because I am in here right now?"

She shrugged her shoulder. "I don't know. I guess sometimes just thinking that way makes it easier. It helps me to escape the reality of my situation. But I do miss you all the time." She said this without looking up. She started to bounce her right foot while looking at the floor.

I didn't know what to say or how to feel. This was my first time meeting her as a young teen, and I just didn't have the words in place to give them to her. I had no idea what she was going through because I had grown up in a household with both of my parents. I mean, they weren't good parents, but they were parents nonetheless. But my daughter was out there alone and without any biological parental guidance.

Before I could respond to try to cheer her up, the guard walked over and told me I had five minutes left until my visit would be over. That crushed my soul.

I stood up and I took my daughter into my arms and held her for dear life. I kissed her cheeks and squeezed her tighter and tighter. I couldn't stop the tears from pouring out of my eyes, and I felt like I was about to lose her all over again.

"I love you, baby, and I promise I am working so hard to get out of here as soon as possible."

She squeezed me back. "I know, Mom. Just keep on doing whatever it takes and get home to me, because I need you."

After they left, I couldn't think straight for an entire hour.

***

That night I tossed and turned in my bunk because I had images going through my brain of my daughter being taken away from me by King Kong. He grabbed her by the arm and started to climb a building with her while she screamed for me to save her, but I couldn't because I was trapped inside a prison cell. All I could do was scream through the bars on the window for the big ape to release her, but of course that was useless.

There was a bright flash that jarred me awake. I opened my eyes just as the guard was finishing his nightly checks. As soon as he walked past, my cellmate Deena climbed down from her bunk and slid into the bed right next to me and started sucking on the back of my neck. I was lying on my side, so she spooned in behind me. I didn't say anything because it was already starting to feel good. She had these real juicy lips, and she did this thing with her tongue that drove me nuts. She knew my neck was my weak spot, and she took advantage of that. I moaned when she bit me. Then I felt her slip her hand under my shirt and onto my bare titties, squeezing the right one and pulling the nipple.

"Mm, baby, you gotta let me get some of this tonight. You put me on hold last night because you said you had a lot on your mind. Well, I hope it's cleared, because I need to taste this pussy, and I want you to fuck me so good I pass out like I always do." She squeezed my titty even harder and humped her crotch into my ass, causing my juices to start flowing.

It was amazing because she was just 19 years old and had gotten to Dwight only six months prior. They had put her in a cell with a big white girl at first, who used to try and rape her every single night. I never really found out if she ever did, but one day they got into a huge fight and both of them wound up fucking each other up really bad. They went to segregation for two months, and when they got back out my old cell mate was being transferred to another place, so she asked the guards if they could put her in there with me. They didn't see a problem with it, and neither did I.

Quiet as she kept, I thought the Puerto Rican girl was fine as hell. I mean, she reminded me of one of those chicks fresh off the island I had seen while me and Avery vacationed in Puerto Rico. This girl had an amazing body with a real big ghetto booty. I didn't know where she had gotten it from, but I couldn't help looking every chance I got. And another thing I liked about her was the fact she had these real big, brown nipples that when they got hard, they stood out a cool inch. I liked to rub them all over my face after I got them nice and wet. I even liked to feel them rub against my clitoris.

When she first moved in, we didn't talk that much, we mostly did our own things and only spoke when we absolutely had to. I didn't want to get to know her, it was obvious she didn't want to get to know me, and I was cool with that to a point. All I knew was she was from the west side of Chicago and she rolled with the Latin Queens, a Spanish street gang of women who ran under the male Latin Kings. I knew this because she had a gold and black crown on her left shoulder; that was their symbol.

I liked her because she was real quiet and she stayed to herself, even in the yard. That was real rare because that's where most of the women did their socializing and rumor spreading. She would be ducked off under a tree reading, or somewhere alone working out, or jogging the track.

Another thing I liked about her was her body, and oh did she have one of those. I loved when we came back from the shower and she would have to change into her other clothes. I play things cool and catch glimpses of her nudity from our mirror in the room. I loved the way her breasts slightly shook as she leaned over to put baby oil onto her legs. I caught glimpses of her backside, and I liked the way it would spread slightly when she bent over. She never wore much around the room other than a t-shirt and panties. One day, before she started doing it, she asked me if I was cool with that. I told her I was and it didn't bother me. From that day forth, whenever we were alone in the room and locked in for the night, that's all she would wear, and I secretly loved it.

Some nights I would lie awake at night in my bed, unable to sleep, and she would always be awake watching her television or studying something for school. I'd start talking to her just so I could see her walk around the room, and then nonchalantly I would be rubbing my kitten under the covers, so softly I barely moved a muscle. I knew she didn't know what I was doing because I had mastered the craft, but one day, after I called her name to get her to talk to me and walk around the room, she let me know she did.

She stood up and looked me right in the eyes and said, "Why don't you sit up so we can talk? Or do you just want to lay back and play with that pussy while I walk around in my panties for you?"

And with that, she sat on the bed next to me and slid her hands under my cover. I had already taken my panties off and put them under my pillow, so she felt between my legs and felt all of my goodies. All I did was spread them for her, and that's when she fingered me for a whole hour while I pulled her top down and sucked on her big brown nipples. After that we started attacking each other every night.

Back to the present, I felt her sucking on my neck and biting me, and it was turning me on so bad. She trailed her hand down and rubbed my booty before sliding it around my waist and down. Her fingers separated my sex lips while her middle finger entered me deeply. I moaned and humped into her hand.

"Mm, you are so wet, mami. You have to give me this pussy tonight. I need it. I am fien'ing for it so badly." She sped

17

up the pace, and I opened my thighs further to give her better access. I had my knee pressed against my ribs as she fucked me with three of her fingers, my chest pressed up against the wall, and her pumping into my ass and pulling my hair like I was a slut or something.

I was already out of breath when she flipped me onto my back and pinned my knees to my shoulders. "Now, I'm about to eat this chochita until it makes me full, baby. Are you ready? Tell me you are ready, mami. Tell me?"

All I could do was moan as she put her whole mouth over my sex and sucked for dear life. I started coming right away, digging my nails into her back. She started talking to me real jazzy then.

"Come for me, bitch. Yeah, come all over my face just like the slut you are. I know you love it," she said, rubbing her face all into my shit.

When she slid her fingers up my backdoor, I passed out for about ten seconds. I woke up with her running them in and out of me at full speed. By this time, I was holding my own knees and egging her on.

I came again, and then I broke up out of her grasp and threw her on the bed facedown, then I pulled her up until she was on all fours. I pushed her panties to the side and exposed her lips, then attacked them as if it was my last meal.

It never took her that long to come. As soon as I hit her sex nipple with my tongue and flicked it for about five minutes, she hollered out and I trapped her pearl with my lips and started sucking her through her climax. I finished off by rubbing her big booty while I lay my cheek against it.

Her pussy smelled ripe, and I loved its odor. I couldn't even lie that I felt some type of way about her. This young girl had me feeling all kinds of funny.

Chapter 2

Alexis

I hated leaving my mother back in that prison, but I had no other choice. I was forced to roll back to the foster home with the same lady I felt like reaching out and smacking. I hated this lady, and even more than that, I wondered if my mother looked at me different because of what she had said about me.

I mean, who wants to meet someone for the first time and find out they are a screw up? It seemed counterproductive to me, but whatever.

I looked out the corner of my eye at the bitch as she drove with her designer glasses on her nose and her expensive pantsuit, and I wondered if this broad thought she was better than me because she had it all put together. Who was she to judge me? She didn't know me from Adam, yet there she was telling my mother things about me to assassinate my character. Something in me was screaming, *Punch her in her shit! This bitch just insulted you in front of your mother!* It took every ounce of discipline I had to not follow my mind's voice.

"You know, Alexis, I think your mother enjoyed your visit. What about you? Did you enjoy yourself?" she asked, pulling into a McDonald's drive-through. "I'm sure they have already eaten back at the Taylors' house, so we'll catch a bite for the road," she said, pulling up behind a moped.

It was just starting to rain outside, and I had to roll up my window to avoid getting water in the car. I lay back in my seat and tried my best to hear Tink on the radio as she sang her new version of Aaliyah's *One in a Million.*

I listened to her order her food. "Yes, that's right. And Alexis, what would you have?" she asked me.

Now, even though I was mad and upset, I wasn't mad

enough that I could not eat. I was hungry, and I had a taste for some chicken nuggets. And if this broad was willing to pay for them, then so be it.

I told her to buy me two twenty-pieces. I would probably be eating on them for the next two days, but I was cool with that, because the Taylors' food sucked, and I mean it was gross. The lady who ran the house couldn't cook at all, so I had to keep that in mind as I ordered. I didn't care that she gave me a crazy look, all that mattered to me was she ordered my food.

We went to Checkers and I got a large fry, and then I made her stop at the gas station, where I got me a two-liter lemon lime pop, and I made sure she paid for it all. I sat in my seat with a sly grin on my face as we rolled back to the foster home.

The Taylors' house was a big crib that had eight rooms, but 16 children. It was ten of us girls and six boys. I got along with mostly everybody, except one girl named Jackie. Me and her had been enemies ever since I'd beat her up in the fourth grade; it was just crazy that years later we would wind up in the same foster home. Her mother had overdosed off of heroin five years prior, and she didn't know who her father was. I think that got to her the most.

There was only four of us teenagers: there was me, Jackie, Leah, and Marshall. The rest of the kids were way younger than us. We were sorta like their parents in a sense because at the Taylor house they didn't give a fuck about us. We were on our own most of the time. The only thing that was promised was three meals a day. Everything else was wishful thinking.

Each kid there was assigned a roommate, and mine was the white girl, Leah. She was a cool brunette who loved to talk and talk all day long. Her face would not stop moving until I would yell for her to shut the hell up. Then she would break down crying and ask me why was I so mean? This would make me feel bad, but only for a moment, because as soon as I apologized she would be back at it again, running her damn mouth. She even talked in her sleep. I could not understand how a person could talk so damn much.

Being that me and Jackie didn't get along, I really stayed to myself. I liked to write poetry to take my mind off of things, so I spent most of my time doing that. I found it to be my oasis. I took pride in my words and I loved the fact they had meaning only to me. I didn't need a reason to talk to anybody.

I have to be honest, though, because like I said before, there were only four of us that were teenagers. The fourth person was Marshall, and I had a thing for him. He wasn't the cutest boy I had ever seen, but I liked him. He was kinda heavyset, but not fat. He had some muscles, and a little short afro. He had a mole on his left upper lip, and I liked the way he talked because he was originally from down south, so he had this real Southern drawl that used to make me hot for him. Any time he talked to me, I for some reason had to squeeze my thighs together to stop that throbbing from down below.

He and I were cool, and I loved to listen to him try to rap because he thought since he was from Atlanta, he was gon' be the next Jeezy. I played the cheerleader role and gave him his props even though I didn't really think he was that good.

He was the only male in the house, and you better believe he knew it, because all three of our little hot asses was always competing for his attention. I think out of all of us Jackie was the worst, because any time she knew he was awake, she had to be all in his face in her little shorts. Jackie was real caramel, with a grown woman's body, and she knew it. She had real natural curly hair and some fat lips. She didn't really have much in the breast department, but her hips and booty made up for that tenfold. Even though I didn't really get along with her, I had to admit she was a good looking female. I mean, I wasn't a hater, but quiet as I kept, I still didn't think she was messing with my business. She was giving me a run for my money, but I refused to give her the title, if you know what I mean.

As soon as I got back to the house, the first person to meet me at the door was Leah. She had a mop in her hand, and I guess they were just finishing up eating and were now doing their chores.

Every time after we ate there we were responsible for cleaning the kitchen and the lower tier of the house. There was an assignment board, and before each meal you were supposed to go and check it to see what your duties would be for the night. But this day, since I didn't eat there, I didn't even go look. I tightened my grip on my bag of food and looked at all of them cleaning and thanked God I didn't have to do that day. I even dug into my bag and popped a French fry into my mouth as if to say, "Ah hah."

Leah came right into my face and started talking a mile a minute. "So, how was your mother? Is she as beautiful as you are? Did you guys hit it off? Did you hug her? Was she happy to see you? When are you going back? When does she get out? I bet it was so cool just being around her. I miss my mother, but then again, I have never met her. I bet she doesn't even think about me. Wow, that makes me sad. I should see my dad this week, but then again, who knows. Oh my god, you went to McDonald's? Did your mom buy that for you? Can I have some? No, maybe I shouldn't because I just ate. Well, maybe a fry or two. No, then again, that is from your mother. It's probably pretty special to you, huh?"

I was literally stuck in place just watching her lips move up and down. How the hell could somebody talk so damn much? This girl was amazing.

I grabbed both of her shoulders and shook her. "Leah,

you're doing it again. Shut the hell up. We'll talk later on tonight about everything, okay?"

"Yeah, Leah, take a break. I know your tongue gotta be tired or something," Jackie cut in as she walked past with a broom in her hand.

I rolled my eyes. "Leah, it's cool. I'll tell you everything tonight. And I'll save you a few chicken nuggets, okay?"

She smiled. "Yeah, that sounds great. Oh, and I'm sorry. I don't even know that I'm doing it when I am."

I gave her half a hug. "It's cool, girl. Don't even worry about it."

Just then Marshall came past on his way out back to the dumpsters. He had two big garbage bags in each one of his hands. When he saw me, he nodded in a *what's up* fashion, and all I could do was smile and lower my head. I didn't know why I liked him so much. I mean, he wasn't all that, but I had to admit I kind of did. I watched him walk all the way from the front room, down the long hallway, and out the back door, then I shook my head to snap myself out of the zone he had me in.

I was on my way up the stairs to my bedroom when Mrs. Taylor started calling my name from somewhere in the house. I thought about ignoring her because I knew her calling my name could not be for a good reason. But I was a good girl. I came all the way back downstairs and navigated around the house until I found her sitting in her room on the edge of the bed, smoking a cigarette. I always hated the smell of cigarettes; I don't know why, but I just did.

I softly knocked on the door and then pushed it in. "Mrs. Taylor, you called me?"

She sat on her bed watching her brand new flat screen television that she had probably bought from caring for us kids, I personally didn't think she deserved it, but then again, my opinion didn't really matter that much.

She had on a silk gown, and her enormous breasts knocked into each other anytime she moved even a little bit. For a black woman she was actually okay looking. She had a little weight on her, but I could tell back in her day she was something to be seen. She wasn't the meanest person in the world, either. I mean, for the most part, she was actually quite fair, but there were times she got on my nerves. I was just hoping this wouldn't be one of them.

"First of all, how was your visit with your mother?" She asked this question without taking her eyes away from the television. That right there told me she really didn't care, so I wasn't about to get to revealing a bunch of stuff to her. I just played it cool.

"My visit was okay, thank you for asking."

She reached her little hand up and started scratching deep within her small afro. "Well, baby, that's nice. I hope you get to see her more often. Every little girl needs their mother." She stubbed out her cigarette in the ashtray. "Do you know when she's coming home?" This was the first time she looked up at me.

I figured she was just trying to see how much more time I had left with them. I knew it was all about money and I represented a paycheck for her and her husband. I wasn't stupid, and I was definitely hip to this broad. "She still has a few years to do before they will consider releasing her, so it looks like you'll have me for a little while longer."

I saw her whole demeanor change. "You make it sound like a bad thing. I hope you don't hate it here too much," she said with fake concern. She even had the nerve to poke out her bottom lip.

"Nall, it's cool here. I just miss my mother is all. I can't wait until we can be together." I switched my weight from one foot onto the other. She was still scratching her afro, then she looked down at her fingernails, and even I saw they were caked with dandruff. I curled up my face.

She popped her finger. "Well, I understand that. But the reason I called you in here is because it is your day to clean the downstairs bathroom. Now, I know you didn't eat here, but I had already did the charts, and it is what it is. So, after you finish your meal, I would appreciate if you would tend to your chores of the night." She lit another cigarette and started flipping through the channels on the television.

I wanted to snap the fuck out. I did not feel like cleaning no bathroom. I just wanted to go upstairs and be alone. At the most I would talk to Leah and work out my thoughts through her listening ears. Sometimes it felt good just to have somebody to listen to me; it helped me to feel more significant. But another reason I didn't want to clean the downstairs bathroom was because us kids weren't even allowed to use it. If nature called and we were downstairs, we would be forced to go all the way upstairs, and I didn't think that was cool at all. On top of that, that bathroom was always the dirtiest. I didn't know what they did in it, but I hated cleaning that bad boy.

She must have saw the look on my face because she immediately put the television on mute and slammed the remote on her bed. "What's the matter, Ms. Alexis,? I know it has to be something because you're giving me that look."

The chick really acted like she knew me, and I hated when a person thought they knew me or they could read me. That was one of the worst things in the world to me, besides actually touching me.

"Mrs. Taylor, I don't feel like cleaning y'all nasty bathroom down here. We don't even use that bathroom, so I don't think it's fair," I said, more sharply than I meant to.

"Little girl, it is not for you to judge what's fair and what isn't. You are supposed to do what I say to, and that's the end of it."

I held my ground. "I don't think that it is, and I need for you to explain to me why we have to clean your filthy bathroom. Why can't you do it? All you do is sit around all day and wait for your husband to show up. You ain't doing nothing. Why can't you do it?"

Her eyes got so big her forehead started to ripple up. "Excuse me?"

"You're excused. Now, can you please answer the question, or are we done here?"

She had the nerve to stand up and walk into my face like I was supposed to be scared or something. She was about three inches shorter than me and probably about 30 pounds heavier. I looked to my right and sat my bag of food down on her dresser. I didn't care what happened between us, but after we were finished I was going to put my stuff in the microwave because my stomach was starting to growl real loudly.

She bumped her breasts into my smaller ones. "Now, I told you to go in there and clean that bathroom. That is an order, and I mean you better do it right away, or else," she demanded, pointing out the door.

I looked down on her and gave a little smirk. "I'm not afraid of you. You're talking about or else? Or else what?" I challenged.

"Or else I'm going to –"

I bumped her. "You ain't gon' do nothing. I know you ain't talking like you gon' put your hands on me, because that show ain't gon' happen. And if it do, we about to tear this whole house up. You must of forgot that for the first twelve years of my life my grandmother and grandfather was beating me every single day. I had to fight both of them, so if you think

I'm about to let your little self put your hands on me without me fighting back, you're sadly mistaken."

She had to be out of her mind, and what I had just told her was the truth. My mother's parents were awful. They beat me every day for nothing when I lived with them from the age of newborn until twelve. I mean, they were the reason I was placed in foster care, because my grandmother had whipped me so bad with an extension cord I had to be rushed to the hospital, and it was there the nurses called DCSF. After an extensive investigation, the state found my grandparents unfit and placed me into the system.

She put her finger in my face. "Little girl, I don't know who you think you are, but you are in my house. And since you are under my roof, you will do as I say, whenever I say it."

I smacked her hand out of my face. "You better get that dirty-ass finger out of my face with all that crust and stuff in it. Ew. Now, I don't have to do nothing you say. You get paid for me to be here, so I'm an asset to you, not the other way around. Don't think I don't understand the system, because I do. I'm not an idiot, just an orphan." I picked my bag of food back up. "Now, like I said, I'm not cleaning up your nasty-ass bathroom. You do it. And if you threaten me again, I will report your ass to them people just like you did me to my case manager. I'll tell them you hit me, and you better believe I can get some kids in this house to say they witnessed it, we can play whatever game you want to, but I ain't cleaning behind no grown-ass woman and man."

And with that I left her room and closed the door behind me. I heard her sitting her big ass back onto her bed because the springs squeaked. When I got into the hallway, the entire house was there and looking at me as if I had lost my mind. Marshall gave me the nod, and I returned it in kind.

***

That night me and Leah sat up talking about my mother, and that was when I found out why she talked so much without stopping. I heated up the McDonald's in the microwave and we got into our PJs, threw a DVD into the player, and had Twilight playing in the background while we chopped it up. I was curious, so I asked her why she talked so much.

She looked a little shaken up at first. She stood up and closed our bedroom door, then locked it. She walked back over to me and knelt down on the pallet we had made in the middle of the room. "Alexis, I never told you this, but my mother had developed a serious addiction to meth when I was only four years old. My father was never present, either because he was in prison or on the run from the law to avoid prison all together. I hated my life." She took a deep breath and swallowed. "So, anyway, my mother started dating this one guy named Mike when I was four years old, and he hated children. He said a child was only supposed to be seen and not heard. That you could not find any place in the Bible where a child actually was allowed to speak. Long story short, he told my mother if they were going to be together, she would have to control me and keep me out of sight or he could not be held responsible for what he'd do to me."

Tears started to roll down her cheeks, and I put my arm around her.

"So, my mother did everything she could to comply with his orders. Whenever he was around, I was forced to stay in my room, and I wasn't allowed to make a sound. She literally wanted me to lay in my bed and not move. Now, because the floors in my room were so weak, every time I would walk across them they would creak, and this would infuriate him.

He would run up the stairs and beat on my door and call me all kinds of names and tell me to shut the hell up, just like you do sometimes." She lowered her voice at saying this, and I felt a dagger go through my heart.

"One day, my mother was out for a job interview and I had awakened having to use the bathroom, so I came out of my room to do just that. I went and did my business, and as I was coming out I bumped into him in the hallway, and that was the start of it all." She was in full tears now. "Alexis, I was five years old, and he beat me so bad I was physically paralyzed for a week straight. My whole body swelled up, and I was forced to stay in my room and away from school until my swelling went down. But it never did, because every day he would assault me in some form. Finally, he locked me into the closet altogether, and my mother couldn't do anything to stop him. I stayed locked up in my bedroom's closet with a bedpan for six whole years. It took six years for him to die of an overdose, and it was only then my mother let me out of the closet. But by that time I was so sick she had no other choice than to take me to the hospital. They found me to be malnourished, sick, and a whole bunch of other things. One day they raided our house out of the blue and they found my mother inside with ten other meth addicts. They were in the middle of making another big batch of the stuff. Long story short, I came here, and I've been here ever since I left the hospital, where I spent six months recovering and regaining my strength."

I wrapped my arms tighter around her and then kissed her on the forehead. She smiled and said something I couldn't understand. I held her face in both hands and looked into her eyes. "Don't worry now, Leah, because you are safe, and you are so beautiful. You are my friend, and I am here for you, do you understand that? If you want to talk on and on for ten years straight, I will listen, okay?" I kissed her on the lips and brushed her hair out of her face.

She sat staring at me for a long time before she leaned her head in and closed her eyes, trying to kiss me again. I was caught off guard by this, but considering the circumstances I rolled with her. Her lips kissed mine and I sucked on them, licking them with my tongue. She moaned into my mouth and I ran my fingers through her long, flowing hair.

I felt her wrap her arms around me, then her hand went up the back of my shirt and she started to unlatch my bra. I felt the back of it open. Her hands sailed up the front of my pajama top, where she squeezed my breasts and ran her thumbs across my nipples.

I had to admit it felt good as hell. My center was all juicy. I opened my legs and squatted down on her thigh so I could rub my crotch back and forth across it to cool the fire that was spreading all throughout my body. She ripped open my pajama top, causing buttons to fly across the floor. I moaned deep within my throat as I felt her lips latch onto a nipple and pull. She even added a little bit of teeth, and that drove me crazy. I didn't know what to do exactly, so I just let her attack me. She started rubbing in between my legs, forcing my pants to go into my lips, and that felt so damn good. I filed it away to try that on my own when nobody else was around.

"Alexis, you're my only friend, and I want to make you feel good like you make me feel. Can I?" she asked with my hard nipple rubbing against her cheek. Her hand was snaking its way into my panties.

Before I could even make up my mind, there was a loud knocking on the door. We scrambled to get away from each other. Leah jumped into her bed, and I did the same thing. The knob on the door started to wiggle, but we played like we were asleep. I felt my juices running out of me and had to clamp my thighs tighter together to subside some of the throbbing that was driving me insane.

"Open this damn door right now or I'm going to kick it in!" we heard the voice of Mr. Taylor say.

I wasn't about to go nowhere, I didn't have any buttons on my top, so I was indecent. If that door was going to be opened it would be all up to Leah. I sat up and reminded her of what she had did to my shirt, I even flashed her a little tittie. She smiled and nodded knowingly. The banging continued until she got out of the bed and opened the door.

"Mr. Taylor, what can I do to help you?" she asked in a cheerful voice.

"Little girl, step to the side. Where is Alexis?"

I heard my name and popped my head up, trying my best to keep my breasts covered. "Why are you looking for me?" I asked.

"There you are, little girl. Get up and get your butt downstairs so you can clean up that bathroom. Now, every time we tell you to do something, that does not leave you room to pop off at the mouth. I want you up this instant, and I'm not playing with you, either."

It was just my luck. Now, how in the hell was I about to explain my shirt or why I couldn't get up in that moment? Dude was already acting like his wife had sent him on a secret mission only he could fulfill. He had his chest poked out and everything. Had I been decent, I would have gotten up and gave him a piece of my mind – but I wasn't, so I didn't. "Alright, Mr. Taylor. Give me a second to get decent, and I'll be right down to finish my chores."

I could see his eyes lower as if he was up to something. "No way. You're going to get up right now with me standing here, and we're going to go down together. Do you understand me?"

I looked over at Leah and she gave me a look of sympathy. I didn't know what to do, so I sat there for a moment trying to calm myself down. "Alright then, let's go." I stood up and pulled my shirt closed and walked out of the room, downstairs into the bathroom with him right on my tail. I grabbed all of the cleaning supplies and mixed my potions for sanitizing.

The bathroom, as expected, was in disarray, and it didn't have the most pleasant of smells coming from it, but what was I going to do? Before it was all said and done, I cleaned up their nasty bathroom and he wound up getting a lot of shots of my breasts because I struggled to keep my shirt closed. It is what it is, I guess.

Chapter 3

Alexis

The next morning, I woke up earlier than usual because I had a lot on my mind. I was thinking about my mother, and I was actually starting to miss her more now that I had seen her. I wondered if she thought about me throughout the day.

I slowly slid out of my clothes and stood before the full-length mirror on the back of the bathroom door. I took a step back and looked at myself from head to toe. My grandparents had made it their business to tell me how ugly I was every single day I lived with them. They told me it so much I started to believe it, and subconsciously I hated myself and my body. I looked into the mirror and tears started to sail down my cheeks. I noted my breasts were not perfect. One was actually bigger than the other. The nipples were way too big and covered more of my breast than I liked. I wished my stomach was flatter. I mean, when I looked onto the television, those girls on there pretty much screamed that girls had to have a flat stomach. If a girl's stomach looked like mine she was not considered beautiful in the media. And being as one day I wanted to be an actress, I knew I would have to get in control of my abdomen.

Another thing I hated about myself was my skin complexion. I was way too dark, and my skin looked as if I had just gotten off of a slave ship. I wished I could have been born lighter, like my mother. I felt that being this black didn't give me a chance in life, and I could never be considered beautiful. To me, I felt as if my skin was a curse, and a constant reminder as to what beauty was not.

I had to wipe my cheeks because I was crying all over again. I took a deep breath and continued to look at myself, praying my image would change; however, I received no such luck. Finally, I stepped away and showered. Just as Leah was coming into the bathroom, I was finishing up wrapping a towel around myself. She came over and kissed me on the cheek.

"Good morning, sister?" she said with morning breath. It wasn't that bad, but it was morning breath, nonetheless.

"Morning," I said, holding my breath and trying to scoot past her back into our room, where I got dressed in the best clothes I could manage.

The Taylors were awfully cheap, so I had to make do with what I had, or what I could steal. I was a prideful person, and my appearance meant everything to me, so, from time to time I would boost clothes with my best friend from school. Her name was Rosie, and she was a saucy little Mexican chick who wasn't to be played with. I loved her, and we had fought back to back numerous times against a whole group of girls.

After I finished squeezing into my Jordache jeans, I slid my halter top over my head just as Leah was coming back into the room in a towel, giving me a look that said she was worried.

"Alexis, we're cool, right?"

I wiggled my right foot into my Jordan shoe and gave her a look that said I was confused. "Yeah, baby. Why would you say that?"

"No, I was just wondering because you gave me a crazy look back there in the bathroom, and you scooted out of there pretty quickly. We usually talk for a while and do our hair together, but today it just seemed a little weird." She unwrapped her towel from around her long hair and shook it out. Once again, I felt my jewel throb.

"Girl, you're tripping. You're my sister, and I love you. The reason I shot out of there is because your breath stunk. I just didn't want to smell it."

"That's it?" she asked, raising an eyebrow.

"Yeah, that's it."

She smiled wickedly and blew out a load of air, and then walked over to me. "So, now that I have brushed, flossed, and gargled mouthwash, do that mean I can possibly get a kiss?" She gave me the puppy dog eyes.

I bit into my bottom lip and walked up on her, grabbing her by the towel and pulling her to me, where I trapped her lips with my own. We made out hot and heavy for about five minutes, and when we were done my nipples were so hard they ached a little bit.

***

I sat in my chemistry class listening to the teacher go on and on about this and that and stuff nobody cared about, and once again I started thinking about my mother. It had felt so good being in a room with somebody who actually loved me, it was a new experience for me, and I wanted to feel it as much as possible. So, instead of listening to him go on and on about things I already knew, I decided to write my mother a letter.

I wrote:

Dear Momma,

I miss you so much, and it felt so good to see you the other day. I think about you all the time and I wonder if you take time out to think about me. Your eyes were so amazing, and I could tell that in them was unconditional love for me. I can't wait until you come home. This world is so cold without you, and nobody loves me, not even myself. Write soon.

Your Daughter,
Alexis

This would be my first letter to my mother, and I hoped she read it. I hoped she really cared about me like she said she did, because she was all I had.

I read my letter to her over and over again until I got enough nerve to say I was sending it

***

At lunch, I walked into the crowded cafeteria. There were probably a few hundred kids there, but I still felt so alone and invisible. I scanned the room until I saw Rosie sitting at our usual table, rolling her head around on her neck, checking her boyfriend just as she always did. I slowly walked over to her and sat my tray down. "What's up, boo-boo?" I said to her.

She saw me and got loud. "Gurl, I'm so glad you're here, mami. This nigga is tripping right now, and I need you to squash this beef between us."

The last thing I wanted to do was get caught up into one of their petty arguments. That never ended well. I was already the third wheel. "Yo, Rosie, that's between y'all, babe. I don't want to get involved. You know how that always ends."

She waved me off. "Fuck that, this nigga gon' say it ain't cheating if a bitch just giving him head. He said since I don't do it, if he can get another broad to do it, it's somehow helping our relationship. Yo, what kind of shit is that, mami? Am I right?"

Her boyfriend, Dexter, gave me a look that said he knew I was about to side with my homegirl. I looked into his handsome, dark-skinned face and those brown eyes and I almost melted. I felt bad for low-key feeling her man, but that nigga was fine and tall. Rosie was always telling me how he put it down in that bedroom, too, and that made me like him even more. I loved his homegirl, but if I had gotten the chance to be that chick on the side to suck his pipe, I probably would have, even though I didn't even know for sure if I knew how to do it. I guess I'd figure it out on the fly.

"I don't know, girl, y'all got a lot of crazy stuff going on. I don't want no parts of that," I said, trying not to look him in the eyes. He already had my nipples swelling up. I did not feel like getting juicy. I got to thinking about funerals, and cockroaches, and all kinds of nasty shit to take my mind off the image of him bending me over that table and fucking me so hard tears came out of my eyes. I started squeezing my thighs together, and it felt like he was actually inside of me. Damn, I was feeling guilty.

"Girl, what? Aw, so you ain't gon' have my back on this one?" She looked hurt. "It's cool." She turned back to him. "Nigga, if I catch your ass fucking with one of these thots around here, we're going to have a problem, and so is whoever the bitch is you're with. No, try me and I'll bring the whole Mexico out to this muthafucka. Sabes que, we'll have on sombreros and ride on donkeys with Mariachi music playing in the background, kicking ass all over the place."

I couldn't help busting up laughing at that. Her ass was crazy, and that's why she was my homegirl.

Dexter rushed off after kissing her on the cheek and muffing my forehcad. I tried to swing at his ass, but he was too fast.

Rosie scooted closer to me and started to whisper. "Mamita, I got the low down on that place on Western. One of my cousins' boyfriends is going to be working there today, and he said it'll be cool if we came through and did a little shopping." At saying this last part, she did little air quotes.

"That depends. Which store are you talking about?"

"I'm talking about the little hood, Saks Fifth Ave one."

My eyes lit up. "You mean the one with all that good stuff in it?" I asked with my eyes big as paper plates.

She nodded her head. "You damn right. We about to be fly as hell. All I need to know is if you're down."

There should have been no question about it. I was all about them clothes, and there was no way I was about to pass up this opportunity. "What time are you trying to ride out?"

"We can wait until school lets out. Just meet me by the football field because I'm parked by it, and we'll roll out from there."

***

I sat in class only looking at the clock. I was ready to blow that joint. I got to imagine myself stepping into some new clothes, and nothing else mattered but that. I was tired of wearing the same stuff over and over. Most of the times we pulled licks because Rosie had the inside information, and that always made things that much easier.

After school let out, I bumped into Leah and Marshall in the hallway. I always found it funny he didn't have any effect on me at school. There he felt more of like a brother, whereas at the Taylors' house he felt tempting.

"What's good, Alexis? You about ready to go? We could all catch the bus together," he asked as his girlfriend Elise slid up on him and wrapped her arms around his waist.

"Yeah, I need to talk to you about something, anyway," Leah added.

Me and her were roommates. I don't know why she didn't understand we had all night to talk, and we usually did. Whatever she had to talk to me about could definitely wait until that night. I was thinking about getting fly, and that was all there was to it.

"Hey, Alexis," Elise finally said.

I nodded. "No, why don't y'all go ahead? I'm gon' catch a ride with my homegirl, Rosie. She need to talk to me about some important things, too. Leah, you and I can talk tonight. I'll meet you two back at home, okay?" I said, throwing my book bag over my shoulder.

Leah looked disappointed, but at that time I didn't have the sympathy to care. I was on a mission, and that's all that mattered.

T.J. & Jelissa

Chapter 4

Alexis

"Alright, girl. Now, all you gotta do is follow my lead. I got everything under control," Rosie said as we walked through the door, causing a bell to ring.

One thing I loved about high-end stores was they always smelled so damn good. They smelled like money, or what I referred to as "Outta Reach."

I did as she said and followed her lead as she walked up to the front of the store where there were two salesmen, one who looked like a stubby Mexican and the other an older white dude. I guessed off the bat the Mexican dude was her peoples, so when she walked up to the counter and started talking to the older white dude, I got confused as hell. I had never met her cousins, so I didn't know if they were older or what, but this dude was.

"Hey, Oscar. I didn't think I would see you here today," Rosie said, leaning on the counter enough to give him a look down her blouse. I had seen her do this same thing so many times before.

He smiled down at her while his coworker gave me the eye and looked me up and down. I smiled weakly and turned my attentions back to her and him as two more customers walked into the store.

I was ready to go. I had already emptied out my book bag, and I had plans on filling it up to the max. I let her work her magic, and when I heard him say they were the only two working, I slowly drifted away from them. To me, she was doing too much talking, I was anxious and ready to get on with the show.

I already knew the aisle I wanted to hit up, and it was full of Ferragamo, Prada, Gucci, and Stuart Weitzman. I walked right up to two Gucci dresses that were about my size and stuffed them into my bag, then I side-stepped to my right and took down two Prada dresses and did the same thing. Under them were some small handbags. I took one and side-stepped down the whole aisle, tearing they ass off. I came out of that aisle and got my Tom Ford game up to par. I looked around and saw Rosie was finally doing the same thing I was.

My book bag was filled to the max, so I left the store, dumped that into her Jeep, and came back in to fill my bag up some more.

I kept replaying certain hip hop videos in my head and going over the lyrics that told me I had to have this kind of fabric across my back in order to be accepted, or to be somebody in general. I was doing this more for the next person than myself because other people's opinions mattered to me so much. I mean, this is the extreme a person would go through when they don't love themselves, and I admitted I didn't, so I wanted to look good so others could validate me.

Rosie left the store and came back, and my second bag was already filled to the max. I was so reckless I went out and unloaded it a second time and came back in to finish getting right. She followed suit as well.

My third bag I filled with underwear and a few pairs of shoes. After I unloaded this into her car, I was good and ready to go. She was just zipping her bag up when I came back into the store and the Mexican dude from earlier grabbed me by the arm so rough it hurt.

I tried to jerk my arm back. "Hey, man, what is your problem? Let me go!" I yelled at him, but all he did was laugh and tighten his grip on my arm.

Rosie looked as if she was ready to crap on herself. "What are you doing, Hector? Let her go," she hollered, still zipping her bag. She slowly made her way over to where we were and tried to pry my arm out of his grip, but that only made him laugh louder.

"You can stop that shit right now. I just watched you two walk out of here with a small fortune. I'm calling the cops, and both of you are going to juvy," he snorted, dragging me across the floor because I had plopped down onto it.

"Oh my god, are you out of your freaking mind?" She looked toward the front of the store. "Oscar, can you please tell him to let her go? He's gone insane or something."

Oscar finished up with the last customers in the store and turned the *open* sign around to *closed*. "I'm sorry, Rosie, but he's the manager. Whatever he says goes."

I could not believe my ears. Hector dragged me to the back of the store and into his office with Rosie right alongside me. He sat us both down in chairs and slammed the door before sitting behind his desk. "Now, where do you get off coming into this store and stealing? Do I come into your house and take your things?" he asked rhetorically.

I was terrified. I kept thinking about him calling the police and them locking me up like my mother. I started to tremble and shake from fear. "I'm sorry. You can have those things back. It's not that serious, we were just being foolish." I did not want to go to jail. They had kept my mother all this time, so I knew I would at least have to stay for some years. The thought of being anywhere for years on end spooked me.

"It's a little too late to be apologizing, little girl. You should have thought of that before you did what you did. Now I have a civic duty to turn you in to the authorities." He picked up the phone.

I looked around the room at all the cameras. I could see Oscar was still out in the front handling customers. The picture quality was so clear I could actually make out the bumps on his forehead.

Hector played us back on video and smiled as he started dialing. I saw myself on screen and got embarrassed. I was acting greedy as hell. I couldn't do nothing but shake my head. My ass was out. They was probably going to make me and my mother roommates; at least I hoped they would. I was gon' need her protection. I was struggling not to cry.

Rosie stood up and snatched the phone from his ear. "You punk! You call the police on me and my homegirl and I'm gon' have my brother shoot you dead in the face. I mean point-blank range, pow!" she said, pointing her finger like a gun.

"What did you just say?" he stammered.

"You heard me, you son of a bitch. You're not going to turn us in, and if you try, you're a dead man."

Oscar came into the office and closed the door behind himself. "What's going on in here?" he asked, worried.

Rosie ran to him and threw her arms around his body. "He's threatening to call the cops on us, and I told him if he does, I'm going to have Javier shoot him in the face. And I mean it, too," she whimpered.

Oscar held her tighter. "Rosie, stop that. You know Javier is in the county jail. Why would you say such a thing?" he asked, looking down at her.

I wanted to drop kick him in the chest. It seemed like Hector was buying the story before he spilled the beans. Now Hector didn't seem worried at all.

Rosie stood in front of Oscar. "Isn't there something you can do?" she asked, looking up at him.

It blew my mind when I saw him reach around and squeeze her booty. His hand rubbed all over it and then slid up the back of her skirt and kept moving. I heard her panties pop and then she inhaled, standing on her tippy toes as his hand moved back and forth under her skirt. She spread her legs until she was standing bow legged with her eyes close.

"There, there, baby girl. You know I won't let him do anything to you. After all, what would your cousin say if I let that happen?'

By this time Rosie was moaning openly and humping backward into his hand while he moved it faster and faster.

The front of Hector's pants looked like a tent, and I couldn't help rubbing my thighs together in my jeans. I wanted Hector to touch me. I needed to feel something between my legs. I was hot, and I needed to extinguish those flames.

He put his hand over his tent and squeezed it. Before I could stop myself, I moaned out loud, never taking my eyes off of his tent. I lifted my left leg and sat my foot on the seat with me, then I put my fingers between my legs. As I watched him squeeze his tent off and on, I rubbed furiously on my kitty until I was humping into my hand. I was so wet my juices were leaking through my jeans onto my fingers.

Oscar bent Rosie all the way over and lifted her skirt out of the way. Then he backed her little ass up until it was against his face and started making loud slurping sounds while she moaned at the top of her lungs. Her face was scrunched up, and she was squeezing her own breasts.

I was so enraptured by what they were doing that I did not even know Hector had popped out his brown penis until I looked up and he was standing right next to me.

"Please, baby, just touch it for me. You're so hot, I would never call the cops on you. Please," he begged, looking me in the eyes.

I was scared at first, and then I got to feeling sorry for him. Well, it was either that or I was trying to make excuses up, because I wanted to do what he was proposing. I wanted to touch his thing. I yearned to do it, especially after he said he wouldn't be calling the cops.

I kept hearing Rosie moaning to the right of me, and that was turning me on. I didn't know how familiar she and Oscar were with each other, but this was definitely not their first go around. When I looked back over to her, he was sliding his dick in from the back and pulling her by the hips back into him at full speed. Their skins slapped together so loud it sounded like somebody was in the room getting smacked on the naked back again and again. I mean, he was giving it to her rough, and she was loving every minute of it because all she did was encourage him.

"Harder, baby! Oh my god, do me as hard as you can. Please!" she groaned as she smashed herself back into him.

That was more than I could take. I looked up at Hector and continued to rub between my legs. "If I do this, you're going to supply me with clothes whenever I want them with no questions asked. Do we have a deal?"

He started to stroke his piece, and I unbuttoned my jeans to further entice him. "Hell yeah, baby, deal. Any time something new drop, it's yours. I promise, mami."

"I'm gon' need some money, too. Ain't no sense in me looking fly if I ain't got no money in my pocket. So, what about that?" I wrapped my hand around his hot piece and stroked it twice while looking in his eyes. "Well?"

His eyes rolled up into the back of his head. "It's whatever you want, momma."

That was all I needed to hear. I started stroking him at full speed, just as Oscar slammed Rosie onto the desk and started dicking her down missionary style. Hector reached and squeezed my breast, and before I could even get into it, he had shot all over my hand.

I wanted to leave right after he did that, but I had to wait for Rosie to finish.

And that she did. She came screaming at the top of her lungs, and then ended the evening by deep throating Oscar so cold even I was amazed.

***

On the ride back home, I got to clowning her. "Girl, I thought you said you don't suck no dick? You could have fooled me. He had his stuff so far in your mouth all I saw was his pebbles," I teased.

"Let's get one thing right: I never said I didn't do it. I just don't do it with Dexter. He ain't ready for all that, plus he ain't keeping me looking this good. When he can step his game up and get me flier than the rest of them, then maybe we can get on this level," she said, turning onto the expressway. "And what was you over there doing with Hector? I couldn't really see because I was doing my own thang." She ran her tongue across her lips.

I blushed and squirmed a little bit in my seat. "I ain't gon' even lie, you and dude had me all kinds of horny. I ain't even know y'all was about to get down until I saw his hand shoot up your skirt. After that I knew you was about to get real freaky."

She laughed and fanned her face. "Yeah, he got some good pipe, and he know how to make it hit all the right places. That's why I love older men, 'cause they know how to put it down." She adjusted her rearview mirror and looked at her reflection, licking the lipstick from her teeth. Then, as if something came to her, she slumped backward and looked over at me while Alicia Keys played on in the background. "Girl, you think you're slick. I asked you what you and Hector was doing while Oscar and I was getting down because I couldn't see you, and you still have not answered me. Now, dish the tea. I'm all ears. Did you suck his dick?"

I almost started choking. I had to hit myself on the chest. I could not believe she had the nerve to say something like that. After all, I had just met him. But, quiet as I kept, had he asked me for it I probably would have tried to do it. They had me feeling so freaky in that little office that in that moment, it was anything goes, but I didn't tell her that.

"Girl, have you lost your mind? You know damn well I don't get down like that. And if I did, it especially wouldn't have been with him."

She smirked. "Um-hmm, yeah. Well, it didn't seem like you was worried about who he was when he was all up in your business. I did see that part, and you did not look like you was tripping at all."

I turned to her and stuck my tongue out while closing my eyes.

***

Back at the Taylors' house, as soon as I walked through the door I could see Mrs. Taylor sitting on the couch in the living room, sewing up one of the younger kids' shirts. I prayed she didn't say nothing to me because I did not feel like having a confrontation with her. But I guess God did not hear my silent prayer because before I could get all the way into the house good, she got to running her mouth.

"Little girl, where the hell have you been?" she asked, standing up with her hand on her big hip.

I rolled my eyes. "I went to an after-school program. I didn't think it would have been a problem," I lied, still making my way toward the stairs.

"Well, the next time you decide to change your schedule on a whim, why don't you try calling somebody and getting permission first."

I placed my foot onto the first step and was glad I had made it that far. I was surprised she didn't ask me why my bag looked all deformed and out of shape, but I was also relieved as well. "I'm sorry, Mrs. Taylor. Next time I will be more responsible."

She grunted, "Oh, you damn right you will. And when my husband gets home he's going to hear about this. You can bet your bottom dollar on that."

I shrugged my shoulders and kept on going up the steps. As soon as I got to the top, I saw Jackie coming out of the bathroom with Marshall behind her. Her hair was askew, and her clothes looked all rumpled up. She also had a big smile on her face that let me know they had been doing something sexual.

Marshal came out close behind with his shirt off, and he avoided making eye contact with me.

"Hey, Marshall. What, you ain't speaking to me no more or something?" I asked, annoyed and a bit jealous. I was hoping Jackie hadn't turned him against me. I didn't care about what they had just did in the bathroom. I could always one-up her on that. I was more concerned about having another enemy in the house, especially one I really liked.

He finally looked up at me. "What? Aw, stop playing. You know it ain't never nothing like that. You know you my girl." He reached his arms out and I stepped into them and felt him wrap them around me. It felt good to feel him against me like that. In that moment I felt secure and cared about.

I looked up at him. "So, what's good with you and Jackie? Y'all talking now?"

He pushed my head back onto his big chest and I could hear the beats of his heart. "Nall, we just cool, fooling around a li'l bit. I wish you would have been here, and then I could have hollered at you." At saying this he trailed his hands down and squeezed my butt.

I backed up out of his embrace. "Boy, you better stop playing. You know you're like my brother. I don't know what she just did for you, but I hope you enjoyed it." I looked around to see if Jackie was somewhere listening. After not locating her, I whispered, "Was it worth cheating on your girl?"

He shrugged his shoulders. "I know if you was my girl, I would never cheat on you." He kissed me on the forehead, and that made me feel special. "When we gon' stop playing and take that walk together?"

He was tripping, and we both knew it. Whatever she had did in that bathroom had him feeling his self, and he thought he could kick the li'l game he had to her on me, but I saw it for what it was. He wasn't on shit, he was just floating on air, and I was gon' let him have his shine. "Marshall, you know I think you're fly, and I love your accent and all that, but I don't want to cross that line with you because right now we got something good going and I look up to you. If we get to messing around together, then you gon' find out I come at a price – a price right now you honestly can't afford. You have to step your game all the way up before you swerve in my lane, because I can't settle for less than the best." I opened up my book bag and showed him all the stolen merchandise.

"When you can scoop me up and take me shopping to stop me from doing this, then...." I took his hand, unzipped my pants, and slid his fingers onto my panty front. He rubbed up and down my lips through them until I could feel myself becoming juicy, then I took his hand away. "When you step your game up, then maybe I can grab onto your controller and play for a minute."

I leaned in and kissed him on the check and walked away,

switching seductively. I don't know what had gotten into me, but I was feeling like a woman, and I knew I'd one day have him eating out of the palm of my hand.

***

When I got into the room, Leah was lying on the bed with her big headphones on, singing silently to herself. She was always trying to bellow out some kind of country music, and what was crazy was she actually sounded good. Sometimes I liked listening to her. It helped my mind to ease a little bit. I walked over to her and tapped her foot. She opened her eyes, saw it was me, and smiled. I ran across the room and closed the door, locking it, then I took my book bag and turned it upside down onto my bed.

Her eyes got as big as saucers. "Oh my god, where did you get all of that from?" she asked, coming over and standing next to me.

I was too busy separating my clothes to give her an answer at first. "Here, this is for you," I said, handing her two short Gucci dresses. One was black and purple, and the other was all black with a hint of blue. I always tried to keep her in mind when I was busting a move. One, because she was my roommate and I didn't want her getting jealous of me and possibly dropping a dime, and the second reason was because we were good friends and I wanted her to look good. Her people didn't care enough to send her any clothes, and I knew how that felt because my mother was locked up, and that prohibited her from doing anything. Although I had other family members who weren't locked up, they never did anything for me, and the Taylors didn't have a clue as to what fashion really was. Even if they did, they weren't about to drop no coins for it. The truth was they spent most of their monthly checks on themselves, so I felt I had to do whatever it took to provide for me, and occasionally for her.

She wrapped her arms around me. "Aw, sis, you didn't have to do this. You know I'll never be able to repay you."

I patted her on the butt to signal I wanted her to release me. "It's not about that. If I got it, then so do you, so stop tripping."

She let my neck go and I started hanging my clothes up in our closet. It wasn't the biggest of spaces, but it helped. Even though it was meant for me and her to share, my clothes covered up about ninety percent of it, but Leah never said anything, and neither did I.

When I turned around she was holding the dresses to her face and hugging them as if they were teddy bears. "You are always spoiling me. There has to be something I can do for you. Come on, think of anything and I'll do it."

I crossed my arms across my chest and started to tap my chin with a finger as if I was mulling things over. "I'll tell you what, you can run me a bath. And then, after I soak for a minute, you can wash my back and make me feel all clean. I mean, if you want to."

But before I could even finish saying that, she had run into the bathroom. I couldn't help busting up laughing.

Chapter 5

Tiny

I was so tired of being in prison. It seemed like every single day was Groundhog Day, because not much changed from one day to the next. I could not believe I had been there for as long as I had. It seemed like it had only been a few years at the most, but seeing my daughter helped my reality set in.

Lord knows I was missing her like crazy, and now that I had finally been given the chance to meet her in person, I knew there was nothing that would stop me from trying to get home to her as soon as possible. They had programs in place that would help sever some of my remaining sentence, and I was on my way to finding out more about them and how I could be made eligible.

Although it was a prison, for the most part it was a rather clean facility. The girls worked in shifts as janitors, and the ones they had now actually liked to clean, which was a good thing because the ones before them were kind of gross and lazy. I had never taken a job as a janitor because I had a weak stomach, and the smallest thing could trigger me to throw up. No thank you.

Every prisoner in our facility was required to work or go to school. I had gone to school earlier in my bid and had gotten my degree in cosmetology, and that allowed me to work in the salon, where I was famous for taking a ratchet-looking chick and turning her into something to see. I was cold with the hair on all levels, and before I had gotten arrested I was going to school for it and had my own chair in a salon. My clientele was about forty people, so I knew my way around.

In a females prison if you're good with hair, then you are considered everybody's best friend because when it was time for girls to go on visits or see their loved ones, parole hearings, or anything of the like, they turned to you to make them look as good as Cinderella. And they would pay you as well, which I always loved because my people didn't send me no money like that, so I had to grind as hard as I could just to get by. I was hoping all of that was about to change because my favorite cousin had gotten out of prison three weeks prior, and he had said all I needed to do was give him a month to get on his feet and he'd make sure I was good. I believed him because I held him down while he was locked up in the past.

I didn't have a whole lot of friends at the place because I tried to stay to myself. Most of the women were all gossip girls. All they did was look for the latest scoop and find reason to down a person to make themselves feel better. Every woman here was going through something they mentally didn't want to succumb to. We were all dealing with losses of some sort, and instead of coming together to console one another, all we did was find ways to tear each other down. It was something I hated and I refused to take part in.

I sat in the long hallway of the prison, watching the heavyset sister mop the floor and talk to herself at the same time. She was wearing an all-gray janitor's suit, and it was two sizes too small on her. She was so big I could actually make out the ripples of her stomach through the coveralls. She had beads of sweat on her forehead, and she had seven ponytail holders around a pony so small most of the holders were hanging on by the tip. I could tell she used that brown hardening gel, too, because otherwise she would have not been able to get her hair into a ponytail. The more she sweated, the more her hair was sticking up on the side like a peacock.

I don't know why I was peeping her the way I was, but I chalked that up to boredom.

She had the nerve to look both ways, and after not spotting

an officer, she lifted one of her legs and let out a fart so loud it sounded like her ass had sat on a microphone before she did it. Then she did it again and fanned her booty, walking in my direction.

Before she could get all the way by me, I spoke up. "Excuse you, but can you not bring that funk over here? I have a very weak stomach, and I can already tell you put in work," I said, rolling my eyes and ushering her away with my hand. It was already too late for me to not smell her. The aroma of her sweaty ass made its way to my nose, and I almost gagged. This broad smelled like she had to shit, and she needed to shower.

She had the nerve to put her hands on her big hips and stare me down like she wasn't smelling like dookie. "Can you mind your business? You don't own this hallway, and if I want to poot all up and down it, I will. After all, I'm the one that's cleaning it, not you."

I was holding my nose by this time and growing more and more irritated by the second. "I don't care whose hallway it is or how much you clean it, the bottom line is I don't want to smell your stanky ass. How you gon' be cleaning the hallway and at the same time polluting it? You smell like you shitted all over yourself and then rolled around in sweat and shame. I gotta be honest with you, you're actually doing more bad to this hallway than good." I still had my nose pinched to emphasize my point.

She dropped her mop and rolled her neck on her shoulders. "Excuse me, you little red-ass girl, but I know you better watch your mouth before I make you. You so damn little that if I get mad enough, I might swallow you and turn you into gas, then poot yo' ass back out. You don't smell so good, either, for the record. You sitting there thinking you better than me when you're not, with your half-breed ass. Yo' momma like getting fucked by white folks, or was it yo' daddy that was fucking yo' white-ass momma? Either way, I'll kick half the cracker out of you and whoop the rest of the nigga, too." She squatted down and raised her left arm in the air and farted with all of her might. This time it went on for a full three seconds, followed by another one that lasted two seconds. This chick had the nerve to turn around with her ass toward me when she did it.

I was so disgusted that I pushed her big booty out of my face and tried to stand up, but the mop she was holding was not completely wrung out, so I wound up slipping on the water from it and busted my stuff.

She started laughing at the top of her lungs, teasing me. She put her hands on her knees and started twerking. I was so embarrassed by this point that I didn't know what to do, not even when she backed her ass up to my forehead and farted again before walking off.

***

I was dusting myself off and plotting how I was going to get her big ass when my social worker opened the door to the hallway and invited me into her office. She was a blond-haired lady of about fifty years old. Her office was small and cramped, and on her desk were pictures of her family. Her husband looked like Colonel Sanders, and her children looked more like her than him. I surmised she was probably a fast girl back in the day and had a few children with different fathers.

I didn't understand why people thought whites didn't get down like that just because they had careers. Trust me, they was just as trifling in some aspects as our people were. She was a good-looking older female, too, and I could tell back in the day she was a fox. She still had that air of sexuality about her.

She flipped her hair over her shoulders and smiled at me. "Now, what can I do to help you?" she asked, looking me straight in the eyes.

I picked up the picture on her desk, the one with her family and her husband. "You have a nice-looking family."

"Why, thank you, Zivial. I appreciate that."

"Is this your husband?" I asked, pointing to the picture of the man that resembled KFC's Colonel Sanders

She nodded. "Yep, that's the love of my life, right there."

She said it with words so dry they needed lotion, even though I could tell that she was being sarcastic. "It's funny how none of your children look like him. You must have strong genes, huh?"

"Must do." She looked down at the photo I was holding and turned her head to the side. "But anyway, let's focus more on you. What can I do to help you this morning? I know you had a visit with your daughter the other day. How did that go?"

I sat her picture back onto her desk and lowered my head the minute she made me think about my baby. I wondered what she was doing at that instant. Was she thinking about me like I was thinking about her? Was she eating, or was she sleeping? Was she safe? I missed her so much it was driving me crazy.

"My visit went pretty good, but it really hurt me to see her leave without me by her side. And that's what I'm here to talk to you about," I said, looking up and catching her take some hair off of her tongue and look at it.

"How so?"

"Well, I would like for you to help me get into a program that would help me sever a portion of my remaining sentence. Is there anything you can do for me?" I asked, wrapping my arms around myself. My stomach was starting to growl because it had been two days since I had eaten anything, and I was starting to feel the effects of my malnourishment.

"Okay, let's see here." She opened my folder on her desk and started flipping through it, reading with her lips quietly. That always irritated me about people when they did that. I felt if a person was going to read something silent enough to be heard, but not enough to be understood, that person should just shut up altogether or read it all the way out loud.

"Um, Mrs. Kyles? That bothers me when people do that, especially when they're reading something about me. So, can you either read it to me or please read it all the way to yourself?"

She gave me a look that told me she was a bit annoyed. "Okay, I have no problem doing that, and I can see how that could be annoying."

She read on in silence, and I bounced my leg up and down on my toes while I waited for her to finish.

"Well, it says here you are already getting day-for-day. They are only making you do fifty percent of your time. I don't understand what more you were looking for," she said, closing the folder.

I cocked up an eyebrow. "Well, my daughter will be 17 in the next couple of weeks, and I feel this is a crucial time for me to be there with her. Now, I know there are programs around here I can enter into that will help me further shorten my sentence."

"You do know your charges are pretty severe, right?" she asked, barely above a whisper.

I felt like reaching across the table and smacking her on the face. How in the hell was she going to ask me something like that as if I wasn't living every single day behind the walls where she was employed while my daughter figured out how to survive in a world so cold? Sometimes I wondered if the people who worked in prison actually got it, or if they just didn't care altogether.

"Of course I realize the severity of my charges, but I didn't kill anybody. That girl was attacking me. She tripped and fell on that knife because she was chasing me. I was trying to get away from her because she was armed. Why don't people get that?"

"Well, it's not for me to say what happened or what didn't happen, or whether you're innocent or guilty. All I am paid to go off of is your files, and your files say that you are guilty and have been sentenced to us for rehabilitation. That's my job, nothing more."

I was getting annoyed. I wanted to jap out on this chick because she was saying that like I was just a number and I didn't matter. It didn't seem like she even factored in my daughter. "You do know I have a little girl, right? And that she's been getting into some minor trouble lately?"

She nodded her head. "Yes, I'm familiar. If you recall it was me who approved for you to visit with her after I heard about her news. I went all out of my way to make sure she was brought up to you."

"Yes, and I appreciate that, but a visit can only do so much. I need to be out there with her. She needs to see my face every single day, and I need to guide her. I hate being here away from her, especially when I didn't do anything. This isn't fair, and I have already lost nearly 17 years of my life from somebody else's mistake."

She pushed on the bottle on her desk and squirted lotion into her hand and rubbed it around and into her fingers. "I hear you, Zivial, but there is only so much I can do. You have to understand every female who comes into my office swears up and down she is innocent. I don't think I have ever met a confessed guilty person in my life," she said, laughing a little.

"I'm glad you think all of this is funny," I said, feeling the tears well up in my eyes. I got to imagining my daughter out there all alone, and it felt like I was being stabbed in the heart. I missed her so much. Her little black face, her pretty features, and big lips she put way too much lip gloss on. I wondered if the men out there were trying to entice my baby into bed. I wondered how many times she was hooted or hollered at, and how that made her feel. I did remember noticing her body was all woman. Physically she was no longer a kid, and she had to have been going through a lot of hormonal feelings. I thought back to when I was her age, and I remembered it being the time I became sexually alive and overtly curious.

"I'm sorry, I didn't mean to make you feel as if I were laughing at you. That was not my intention." She took a deep breath and blew it out.

I sat across from her with my head down and feeling defeated. I wanted out of that place, and I didn't know how much longer I could stay in there without going crazy. It was getting to the point where every time I woke up, I felt a strong wave of depression overcome me. I wanted to go home.

We were silent for a long time. She kept on lotioning her hands, and by that time they had to be saturated. I kept my head down, feeling sorry for myself.

"Zivial, I'll tell you what. Let me talk to the warden to see if I can get you in to be his trustee, and that way you can at least work your way on out to a work release program in the community. Now, he conducts his own interviews, and if after he looks at your file he calls you for one, then nine times out of ten you'll get the job. Just let me work my magic and you get yourself together. I can't promise you anything, but I will do all I can. I will promise you that. How does that sound?" she asked, standing up and extending her hand.

Now I was feeling a whole lot better. I had never actually

seen the warden, but from the way he had changed the rules at our prison to better suit us, I felt he was kind of cool. Not many did that, so I felt if I could get the interview, I could get him to take me on as his personal trustee. Every last one of the warden's trustees had left the prison and went into the community after working for him, so this was the opportunity of a lifetime.

"Please do all you can. I promise you will not regret this." We shook hands and I stood up, almost hysterical. I tried to hurry up and get out of that office before she changed her mind.

I was halfway out of the door when she stopped me. "Oh, and for the record, Zivial? Those kids aren't my husband's." She winked at me and sat back in her seat, smiling.

T.J. & Jelissa

Chapter 6

Tiny

I was walking around the prison with my head in the clouds all week, praying I got called up into the warden's office for an interview. It was all I could think about with the exception of Alexis. I thought about her all the time. I mean, everything reminded me of her, especially the teens on television. I wondered how much of her personality was like those on sitcoms or documentaries I had watched. I hated missing out on her life. I felt our relationship would never be strong because of how long I had been away from her. How could I even step in to try and be a mother to her when I had never been there? Would she listen to me or laugh in my face? Had she had her period yet? Of course, she had to. I mean, she would be 17 in a few weeks. Wow, how could I have missed that? I wondered who had taught her about all of that. Did she hate me for not being there? Was it wishful thinking to assume we could have a strong relationship one day? I hoped we could.

I was feeling so low and in the dumps, all that week waiting on the warden's call, when the best thing that ever happened to me could have: my cousin Roman came up to see me. When I saw his name on the paper they handed me, I nearly ran all the way to the visiting center without getting dressed first, but I didn't. I got dressed and double-timed up there so I could see him. I was fien'ing to see my blood, too.

When I came through the door, he didn't even notice. He was too busy loading the table up with snacks. He looked real fresh in his Roberto Cavalli fit and the black-and-white Jordan #3s to match. He had his bald head clean and shining, and I could tell he was out there giving them broads all they could handle.

I walked up to him while he had his back turned and tapped him on the shoulder. "Excuse me, sexy man, but have you seen my cousin?"

He turned around and smiled, looking all good with his goatee lined up and stuff. "Hey, cousin," he said, wrapping his arms around me and hugging me close.

It felt so good to be in his embrace. This was my favorite cousin, and we had always been close. I tried to hold him down as much as I could before I had gotten locked up. Since I had been down, he'd had a few females he was messing with hit my books from time to time, or any time they hit his he made sure they gave me half of it. It was because of him I wasn't doing too bad in there, so he was my heart.

"Oh my god, I have missed you so much. And you smell so damn good," I said, sitting down across from him. All eyes were on us, and I could see the other prison bitches jocking my people. They clearly picked up that I didn't kiss him on the lips, which let them know he was fair game or probably a family member. Now, in prison this was the worst, because after I left that visiting room every broad in the place was about to be at my doorstep trying to get hooked up. I didn't have time for that. I mean they were staring him down.

"Roman, I need you to do me a favor."

He frowned up his handsome face. "Okay, what's that? You know I got you."

I looked around and them hos was still looking like he was naked or something." I need you to let me kiss you so these hos don't be all on my doorstep later tonight trying to get hooked up. You know how crazy I am. I would have been snapped on one of these bitches, for real."

He started laughing. "All right, that's cool, but don't be trying to stick your tongue all down my throat and shit."

"Shut up."

I grabbed him by his shirt and our lips came together for about thirty seconds. I mean, since I was acting, I was making the best of it. It was a mixture of that and the fact it had been so long since I had kissed a man. I almost forgot who he was to me because I started sucking on his lips and moaning. He pushed me away when I tried to snake my tongue in there, and that snapped me out of my zone. I was breathing hard as hell, and he was, too.

"I told you, I don't like that tongue shit. Yo' ass getting too carried away," he teased, moving all funny in his seat.

I found myself looking down and noted he was trying to hide something in his lap. "Boy, I know that ain't what I think it is," I said, trying to move his hand out of the way.

"Girl, g'on, stop playing," he said, smacking me on the hand and looking embarrassed at the same time.

"Uh-huh. Yo' ass done got to feeling some type of way, huh?" I crossed my leg over the other one and he looked off.

"Nall, it ain't that, but you know I'm just getting home from doing a short bit, so that feminine thing still getting to me. I know we blood, but my little homey in the basement don't know the difference, if you know what I mean."

We both busted up laughing.

"So, why you ain't tell me before you came out here? You got me looking all rough and shit."

He ran his hand over the top of his head and smiled, making both of his dimples pop out. "I don't care how you looking. I wanted to see you, so as soon as I was able to, that's what I did. I also put two gees on your books, and I sent you a bunch of clothes and stuff. You told me you wanted a pair of Js, so I just sent you two pair. I made sure I got the socks and all that to match, and you should get your pictures today that I took for you."

He opened the cap to his pop and took a long swallow. I watched his Adams apple move up and down, and my eyes got misty.

"Damn, you making me want to kiss you again, li'l cousin. You did all that for me?" I felt my heart fluttering.

"Man, stop playing. I told you I had you as soon as I got out, and I meant that. I'm gon' make sure you stay straight for as long as I'm out here. That's my word. I remember when you was a teenager and you use to have that white girl hitting my books up. What was her name?"

"Amber."

"Yeah, her. She was writing me for a minute, too, sending me naked flicks and shit. I appreciated all of that. Then, when you got your li'l salon job, you kept me right. That may have been a li'l while ago, but I still remember it as if it were yesterday."

I was sitting there crying like a big-ass baby. He always knew how to pull on my heartstrings and break me down. I loved my little cousin so much.

"Babe, why are you crying?" he said, reaching across and grabbing my hand in his. "I thought you would be happy if I came out to see you."

I shook my head. "Nall, it's not that. It's just that you always make me feel so loved. I'm so glad you are here right now."

He got up, came back, and handed me some Kleenexes to wipe my face. Then he leaned down and kissed me on the forehead. "I'm happy I'm here, too, but I don't want you crying no more. You know you're like my rock, so if I see you being all soft, then what am I gonna do?"

I took a deep breath and tried to straighten up. "But thank you, though. You know you didn't have to do all of that."

"It's cool, because while I was locked up you know I was

writing them books and shit, and I got this li'l company that been publishing them one-by-one. I just got my first royalty check, so you know I had to hold you down. I'ma take the other half and bust a move with it until they get my other royalty check off to me."

I did remember him talking about some books he had wrote. I had never seen one, but I could tell by his letters he was a writer. That inspired me, because I had always wanted to write and tell my story, and I told him that.

He looked guilty and lowered his head, then it took him a full five minutes to look me in the eyes. I had to pop him on the leg before he did that.

"What's the matter? Why you not looking at me right now?"

He shook his head. "Because I got a confession to make, and I don't want you to get mad."

People should know when a person tells me that, it only makes me mad ahead of time. So, when they finally decide to tell me what the problem is, I wind up two times madder than I would have been if they had just come out with it. "So, dish, then. What are you waiting for?"

He rolled his head around on his neck. "I may have already written a book about what happened with you and got it published. And if that's so, would that make you mad?"

I sat back in my chair with my eyes bucked wide open. "I don't understand what you're talking about."

"Well, you know how you wrote me all them letters over time? I put all of them together and wrote a book about it called *Loyal to the Game*, and that joint is hot. One of the homies down south in Georgia got a publishing company, and he been fuckin' with me. And that book been flying out like hot cakes, even on the line."

Now I felt offended. "Why haven't I got a copy yet?

Especially if it's about my life.?"

He started laughing at this, and from there on we just shot the shit and reminisced a little bit. Everything was going good until he asked me about Alexis.

"So, how is she doing? And when can I go over and meet her?" he asked as he sat my microwaved food down in front of me that he had just heated up.

I felt my stomach flip over. "I don't know, but her birthday is next week. Maybe you could pop up on her and surprise her."

He rubbed his chin and looked as if he really considered it. "But wouldn't it be weird if I did that, because she has never seen me before?"

I bit into the hot ham and cheese vending machine sandwich and burned my mouth. I dropped that sucker immediately and screamed like somebody was trying to kill me. My cousin thought that shit was funny because he fell out of his seat laughing, rolling around like a damn fool. I didn't think it was funny at all. I was busy trying to wipe my tongue on a napkin to subside some of the pain.

I kicked his foot. "Get yo' monkey ass up and sit in that chair. You're embarrassing me," I said, although he really wasn't. That boy was just crazy, and he was always finding a reason to laugh at me for something.

He slowly made his way to his seat, holding his stomach. His eyes had turned red as hell and he had tears rolling down his cheeks. "Yo, I just told you it was hot, and you still took that big-ass bite. That cheese stuck to your upper lip. That's what got yo' ass, ain't it?"

"Shut up!" My lip was burning, too, but I wasn't about to admit that to him.

"Aw, poor baby. Want me to kiss it for you?" He closed his eyes and stuck his lips out.

68

I picked up the sandwich and was about smash it into his face, but he opened his eyes up just in time to back away."

"Damn, that's what we do? Just tell me about my li'l cousin and I'm out of here 'fore you try and hurt me and shit." He looked a little upset now.

I felt bad. After all, he was only playing. I didn't want to ruin a good thing after he came all the way out there for me. "I'm sorry, babe. I was just a little salty at you laughing at me. I'll give you her address and write her a letter to let her know you'll be stopping by. I think it would be a great idea, though."

T.J. & Jelissa

Chapter 7

Alexis

I woke up the morning of my seventeenth birthday feeling sick and like I didn't want to get out of bed. What was the use, anyway? I knew nothing special was going to happen; it was just about to be another day at the Taylors' house. I could not wait until I turned eighteen, that way I could just be a long way away from them and everything else that made me unhappy, and by that I meant life in general. I would have loved the chance to see my mother that day, but I knew it wasn't going to happen, so I really felt like what was the use of getting out of bed?

I must have lain there for about two full hours listening to everybody move about the house. I figured that none of the even had the slightest idea that it was my birthday. I mean, I never brought it up, and I'm quite sure that even though the Taylors had it down on an application form, they wouldn't entertain the thought of giving me a party or taking me to see my mother for my special day.

Jackie knocked on my room door and let herself in. "Uh, Alexis, you have a phone call. I don't know who it is, but she sounded pretty impatient. You might want to talk to whoever it is about manners." She rolled her eyes and dropped the phone onto my dresser. Somehow the speakerphone function was triggered. I could hear Rosie saying, "Hello, hello? Is anybody there?"

"Yeah, Rosie, I can hear you, but hold on." I picked up the phone and placed it to my ear. "Go ahead, I'm here now."

"Feliz cumpleaños, or happy birthday, chica!" she screamed into the phone. "I'm on my way over to get you right now, and I don't care what the Taylors are talking about.

You're rolling with me, and we're going to have you a nice party. I got some people from school coming over, too, so get dressed, mami! I'm out."

I heard the phone click dead, and I couldn't help shaking my head, laughing. That girl was crazy.

I took me a nice hot shower after I used the bathroom, then I got dressed in a nice Prada cheerleading lookalike outfit. It was all black and purple and hugged my body like a second skin. I felt real feminine in this outfit, and I knew it would cause me to turn heads. I stood in front of the mirror on the back of the door and checked how it made my butt look, and I had to admit I was stacked. All I had to do was oil my legs and do my hair and I was good to go. My toes were already painted, so I was good

After I got myself together, I sprayed on a little J.Lo perfume I had taken from Boston Store, and then I was good to go. I grabbed my purse and made my way downstairs. I didn't even look behind me. I didn't care who was there or who didn't want me to do what. I went and stood on the porch, waiting for Rosie's Jeep to pull up.

Leah must have looked out the window two times before she built up enough nerve to come out onto the porch with me. It was a real hot summer day, and the humidity was just starting to kick in. There were flies around everywhere, and they were driving me nuts. I swatted one away and was about to step on it when she came onto the porch and wished me a happy birthday. She handed me a little box, which I took and opened. Inside was a diamond necklace.

"I hope you like it. I have been saving my allowances for six months just to get it for you."

I was taken aback. I opened up my arms for her to come into them, and we hugged tightly, followed by me kissing her on the cheek. "Thank you, baby. This means a lot to me. I can't believe you actually remembered."

She hugged me tighter. "How could I forget the day the prettiest girl in all the world was born? It is the greatest day of the world."

I felt her starting to nuzzle into my neck and I knew she was about to start sucking on it, but then we heard Rosie's Jeep a short distance away banging a track by Nikki Minaj, so we broke apart just as she pulled up to the curb. Leah gave me a look that said she was jealous, but I didn't have time to baby her because Rosie had parked and ran up the stairs with what seemed like ten shopping bags. She dropped them at my feet and hugged me so tight I couldn't breathe. "Happy birthday, baby! I love you so much, and all of these are for you. Now, take them upstairs and let's get out of her. Vamanos, mami," she said, patting me on the butt.

Leah helped me pick them all up. We stumbled up the stairs with all eyes on us. I didn't care, I just wanted to get those bags into my room and get back out that door as fast as I could. I threw them into my closet and tried to close it, but that wasn't happening. Finally, Leah said she had it, and that was a relief. I turned on the balls of my feet, trying to get out of there, but she pulled me to her and before I knew it we were making out. She was squeezing my breasts and rubbing in between my legs. I couldn't help but moan and hump into her hand to feel her better. My tongue twirled around hers and we sucked on each other's lips passionately.

She started sucking my nipples through my top. "When you come home tonight, can you promise it will be just you and I all night?"

She bit into my neck and slid a finger into me, and all I could do was nod. "Yeah, baby."

We broke away from each other when we heard Jackie's voice. "Your friend told me to tell you to…." She stopped.

"Well, what do we have here?" she asked, amused and crossing her arms across her chest.

I was too busy trying to straighten my clothes to say anything, and Leah had turned redder than a crayon. I brushed past her and out of the room door. I must have flown down the stairs on my way out the door when Mr. Taylor called my name. I was a split hair away from ignoring him, but it would have been too obvious. "Yes sir?" I asked, clearly annoyed.

"Alexis, I know it's your birthday, and we don't mind you going out for a while, but you have a relative who is on his way over to see you. Unfortunately, you will not be able to go anywhere until that happens. This is out of my control."

A relative, and a male. I wondered who in the hell he was talking about. I knew it couldn't have been my father because he was all screwed up in the head. We didn't have any type of relationship, so I couldn't see him driving over from the projects to see me. I was confused. "Did they say who it was?"

He shook his head. "All we were told is it's family and they were approved to meet you."

I did not feel like meeting somebody new at that time. I was ready to go kick it with Rosie and get my groove on at the party. It was sure to have a lot of hot guys there, and I couldn't wait to dance. I didn't understand why I couldn't meet this new person at another time, and I expressed this to Mr. Taylor.

"I don't make the rules, honey. I am just forced to enforce them. So, you can wait on the porch with your little friend, but you cannot leave until he shows up. I'm sorry," he said, lighting up a cigarette.

***

When I stepped onto the porch, Rosie was there waiting for me with her hand on her hip. "Really, you gon' keep me

74

waiting out here in this hot-ass sun with nothing to drink? You didn't even ask me if I wanted to step in for a minute. What type of manners were you raised with?" She shook her head and started to walk down the stairs. When she turned around and saw I wasn't following her, she stopped. "Now what's the matter? Keep in mind that this is starting to get annoying." I could tell she was serious.

I started to fan my face with my hand. "Well, unfortunately, I have to wait until my family member shows up. From what I'm told, he's on his way right now. After I meet him, then I can leave. I'm sorry, babe."

Rosie dropped her shoulders and pouted. "Why is this happening to us?" She sounded like a little kid.

I had to laugh a little, but I did feel how she felt. I wanted to get up out of there, but I didn't feel like arguing with Mr. Taylor. Most of the times when he got mad he always said things to make you feel worse than you were already feeling. I didn't really have a problem with him, but he did get on my nerves a little bit.

Rosie turned around and slowly walked up the stairs. I held my arms out for her, and she walked into them. "Aw, poor baby. It's going to be okay. We'll be out of here in a minute, I hope."

She took a step back. "Can't we at least wait in my Jeep under the AC? Because it's hotter than hell out here."

I shrugged my shoulders. "I don't see why that would be a problem. Come on." I followed behind her and we both climbed into her Jeep. As soon as she cut the AC on, I was feeling a whole lot better. I didn't like the fact my clothes was trying to stick to me, I felt a little uncomfortable, but the air was making me feel better.

Rosie let her seat all the way back and closed her eyes. "So, who is this person again that we're waiting for?"

I followed suit and let my seat back a little as well. "I don't know. They didn't say who he was, only that we were related and he had gotten proper approval prior to this visit to see me." I was racking my brain, trying to think of who it could be. I was hoping it wasn't my grandfather. After all, what would he want with me at this time? He had abused me enough, both emotionally and physically, him and my grandmother. If I never saw them again for the rest of my life, it would not bother me one bit. In fact, I hoped I never did. When I thought back on all the things they had taken me through, it literally almost broke me down. I did not understand how a child's grandparents could feel about them the way mine felt about me, especially when I had never done anything wrong to make them feel that way. They were a huge portion of the reason I hated myself to a fault.

Yeah, I hoped it wasn't my grandpa. It could be anybody other than him and I would be okay with that.

The AC felt good on my face. I had a hard time sleeping the night before, and Rosie wasn't saying much, so before I knew it I had dozed off.

I woke up to her nudging me on the shoulder. "Alexis, girl, get up. I think this is who they're talking about. And if it is, you need to see if he looks familiar to you."

I stayed low in my seat as we watched the Range Rover pull up behind us, and a tall man got out dressed to the nines in an all Tom Ford fit, except for the Space Jam Jordans he had on his feet. His neck had a little gold around it, and from what I could see he looked good as hell. I was hoping he wasn't no kin to me because I found myself choosing off the rip. There was this twenty-something-year-old female who stayed next door to the Taylor house, and I got to wondering if maybe he was going to head up her porch, but to my surprise he walked right up our steps and knocked on the door.

Now I felt my heart beating all fast, and I was starting to get shy. Rosie could not take her eyes off of him. It was like she was eating him up from a distance, and I had to admit I was, too, which was weird because he had to be at least ten years older than us.

The door opened to our house and I saw Mrs. Taylor come out smiling all in his face with her big old titties. Clearly she had neglected to wear a bra because I could see her nipples through her shirt from where I sat. I could tell the man, whoever he was, was trying his best to be respectful.

Finally, she pointed to Rosie's Jeep, and I felt my heart drop.

T.J. & Jelissa

Chapter 8

Alexis

As he was coming down the steps, I was rolling down my window. He walked up to it and smiling, looking even more fine up close. "Excuse me ladies, but which one of you is Alexis?" he asked, and for the first time I was able to tell his whole bottom row of teeth were covered in gold.

Rosie spoke up right away. "That's me. Why? What's good? We can ride off right now," she said, looking like she wanted to devour him whole.

I gave her a look like she was nuts, and all he did was laugh. "No offense, but you look a little too Spanish to be my little cousin. Not saying that is a bad thing, it's just her mother told me she was the most beautiful complexion in the world, and I always considered that to be chocolate." He trailed his eyes to me.

I couldn't believe how much I was blushing, and at least now I knew what he was to me and who had sent him.

Rosie wasn't about to give up. She was leaning all over my lap, trying her best to get into his grill. "I'm saying since we ain't family, our potential is limitless. How about you make me your baby mother, 'cause I'd rather be that than your cousin anyway," she said, serious as hell.

He flashed us both dimples as he started laughing. He even took a step back to bend over while Rosie looked at him like she was dead serious. He walked back to the window. "Li'l momma, you gon' get me in trouble. Plus, I can't be focusing in on that right now. I'm supposed to be here for her. So, what do you say, Alexis? You gon' step into my truck so we can talk a little bit?"

I was somewhat skeptical. "Who sent you?" I asked,

looking him in the eyes. If it had been my grandparents, I didn't care how fine he was, I wasn't going with him.

"Your mother is my favorite cousin, and we been holding each other down for a minute now. I been wanting to meet you, but I just got home myself from doing a tour of duty, so to speak."

As soon as I figured it was my mother who sent him, I felt safe enough to walk to his truck. As I was on my way to stepping inside, Rosie stuck her head back out of her window. "Hey, don't be trying no funny business with her, either. If you wanna try anything like that, then I'm right here waiting. You got that, Papi?"

He lowered his head, laughing as he helped me step into his big truck. "That girl something else."

His truck smelled brand new, and he had flat screens all around inside of it. Bellowing out of the speakers were Li'l Dirk and Chief Keefe, two of my favorite artists. I felt a little uneasy, especially when he slid into the driver's seat and looked over, smiling.

"Girl, you are a beautiful chocolate version of your mother. That's what's up, though. What I want to do is roll around the block a few times just so we can talk, or would you feel better if we stayed parked?"

I really didn't mind rolling around with him, but I had to consider I had Rosie waiting on me, and that would have been all kinds of rude, so I told him that.

"Well, what if she roll out, and me and you go catch a bite to eat? Then in an hour or so I drop you off at her crib and y'all can continue your day?"

I thought about that for a minute, and I guessed that could work, but I wanted to make sure my friend was straight first, so I had him pull up on the side of her Jeep and I rolled down my window. She did the same when she saw us.

"Say, babe, I'm going to meet you at your house in a hour or so. I'm going to see what's good with my cousin, then I'll be over there Is that cool?"

Rosie looked disappointed at first, but then nodded in understanding. "Yeah, mami, that's cool. But you make sure you bring him along with you so I can keep on shooting my shot. I'm on his chocolate ass, and I ain't about to stop until I got a mixed kid crying in the house." She started up her jeep and waved at us. "Bye, baby daddy. I'll see you later with no panties on, I'm just saying."

We pulled off with both of us laughing. As soon as we could not see her Jeep anymore, things got a little tense.

"So, what is your name?"

"Damn, I ain't even tell you that. That was rude of me. My name is Roman, and yeah, I'm your third cousin. My father and your mother are first cousins, but me and her cool like siblings."

I nodded. "You said you just did a tour of duty. Was you speaking in jest, or were you actually serious?"

He sped through a yellow light and switched over two lanes to get on the highway. Once there, he put his foot on the gas. "Nall, what I meant is I just got out of prison from doing a few years."

"Okay, so what did you do?" I wanted to know because it seemed like everybody in my family was always getting locked up for something or the other.

"I'ma let you know right now, Alexis, that for as long as I know you, I will never lie to you. I want to establish that in the beginning. So, from here on out, don't ask me questions about anything you don't want to know the truth to, okay?"

I nodded. "That's a bet. I don't like liars, anyway. So, what did you do?"

He took a deep breath and blew it out. "I had to hit up this

81

one nigga that clapped at me while I was with my little sister. I caught him up in the Stateways slipping and had to put that iron to him. I wish I would have done things differently, but it is what it is."

I could see what we were talking about was affecting him in a major way, but I wanted to keep the spotlight on him, so I kept going. "Well, did you kill him like they say my mother killed that other lady?" For this answer I turned all the way facing him. I wanted to see his every reaction.

He nodded. "Yeah, I clapped him down. He bodied."

I shrugged my shoulders. "Oh well. I guess that's a normal part of life, being in Chicago."

We wound up rolling out north, where we snatched up some homemade subs from Gotto's. He parked close by the lake and we sat on the hood of his truck and talked. "So, now that you know where I am, what's going to change?"

He tried to chew the food in his mouth a little faster. After he swallowed and chased it down with a Sprite, he wiped his mouth. "Well, I personally want you to come and live with me until your mother gets home. I got a nice-sized crib, and you'd have your own room and your own space. I'd let you do your own thing. Financially, I can afford to care for you and keep you straight. I did a lot of saving when I was in there, and I busted a lot of moves that got me into a nice position to be able to be there for you. But that's all up to you."

All I was thinking about was getting the hell away from the Taylors' house. It's like my cousin had fallen out of Heaven and was sent to rescue me. I was so anxious about living with him I couldn't contain myself, but I had to keep it ladylike. "Are you sure your ladies wouldn't mind me being there? I mean, I don't want to cramp your style or nothing like that."

He shook his head. "I don't live with no women. The only

female that held me down while I was in there was your
mother, so she's all that matters, with the exception of you. I
mean, I do got a few female friends, but you would definitely
take precedent over them."

He had me feeing all good and stuff, but I wondered if he
would feel that way once he got to know me. I felt there was
something in me that chased people away over time, and I felt
I was destined to be alone and unloved. He seemed as if he
genuinely cared about my mother, and that radiated onto me.
His home sounded lovely, and secretly I could not wait to
move out of the Taylor house.

"Roman, if you can make it happen, I would love to stay
with you. This would be the first time I was placed somewhere
I wanted to be. I don't think my mom would send you to me
if you weren't a good guy, so what do I have to do?"

He wrapped his arm around my shoulder, and I felt so
secure in that moment. He smelled so good, and I could feel
his muscles through his thin shirt. There was no doubt in my
mind that if it came down to it, he could protect me, and that
made me feel special.

"Don't you worry about nothing. I got this. Before I take
you over to your friend's house, I got something for you." He
helped me slide off his hood, and then he opened his truck
door and crouched down, digging way under his seat. After
what seemed like an eternity, he pulled out a Crown Royal
purple bag, went inside it, and handed me a bundle of money.

"This is yours, and I don't want you asking nobody for
shit. This is $3,500, and that should hold you off for a little
while until I can get you away from these people. If you need
anything, you hit my phone and I'm gon' be there for you, do
you hear me? Matter fact, I want you to buy a phone with some
of that money. That way we stay in contact at all times."

I didn't know what to do. I was standing there with all

those hundreds in my hand and him looking at me and my mind just froze. Finally, he leaned in and gave me a big hug, followed by kissing me on the forehead.

It was the first time in my life I ever felt like a princess, and that made me cry a little. When he saw this, he crouched down, took my hand and kissed the back of it, stood up, and pulled me to him. We stayed that way until my tears stopped.

***

"Girl, shut up. You telling me he just gave you all of that, and he didn't tell you what to do with it?" Rosie asked, flopping onto her bed on her stomach.

I was sitting Indian-style, facing her with all of those hundreds all over my lap. I could still not believe he had given me so much money. I wondered if he was rich, or if he had robbed somebody, but then again a part of me didn't even care. I was too busy trying to get myself to view him as my cousin, but I was finding that so hard. No one had ever shown an interest in me, or cared about me enough to take me out of foster care. This was new territory I was treading, and it had me spooked. When I was eventually set to move in with him, I didn't have the slightest as to how I would handle that. I didn't really understand the concept of family because I had never had any in my life. What I saw was a man who cared about me enough to take me away from my current pains, and that made me feel some type of way.

"Girl, I ain't lying. He told me to just make sure I bought a phone. That's it, and I did that right away."

Rosie rolled onto her back. "Damn, I gotta get his semen in me. I'm about to trap that nigga. He gon' give me some kids, fuck that." She looked like she had zoned out, staring at the ceiling. "If he can just drop damn near four bands for the fuck of it, then he got stupid paper somewhere."

I was sitting there on the floor, listening to her and feeling jealous as hell. I felt like she was plotting on him already, and he had just come into my life. I was not trying to lose a new relative when I didn't have any like that to begin with. "Rosie, get off of that shit. That's my people. We ain't about to bust no moves on him, especially since he talking about taking me away from that place. Not only that, but him and my mom are really cool. I would be crossing both of them."

She sat up on her bed and looked down at me. "I am not plotting on him, but I'm gon' get me some of that pipe. I could literally see it through his pants when he was walking. Homie is strapped, and I see his chocolate ass all over me. Damn, I can't wait." She put her big pillow between her legs and started humping it while laying on her back.

"Girl, chill. Let me get to know him first. Damn, he just came into my life, and you already trying to jump his bones. Step back." I said this more harshly than I actually meant to.

She sat up again and looked at me. "Holy shit, you like him. I can see that all in your face. Bitch, you like that nigga, and didn't he say he was your family?"

I didn't say anything for a while. I was trying hard not to blush. I mean, it couldn't have been more than a harmless schoolgirl crush, but I still wasn't about to let her in on that secret. "You tripping. Don't nobody like him like that. I just don't want you running him away already. Trust me, it ain't nothing more than that."

T.J. & Jelissa

Chapter 9

Alexis

Rosie's mother allowed her to use their whole house for my party, and I had to admit my homegirl had gone all-out for me, because she made sure the whole pad was decked out with banners and balloons. They went crazy on the food aspect, weed, and we even had some wine coolers her mother approved. I had to admit I was feeling quite special. I kept hugging my friend and trying to give her money for everything, but she would not accept it.

What she did allow me to do was take her out to get an outfit for my party. One thing about us females, when it comes down to clothes, we'll never turn down the offer to receive more. Trust me on this. So, I felt like this would be an easy way for me to repay her. I just didn't like people doing things for me without me giving them something in return, I felt indebted for some reason, and my conscience would not be cleared until I spent on her roughly the same amount she and her mom had on me.

We could have easily hit up our old friends Hector and Oscar for clothes for free, but neither one of us felt like dealing with them, so we decided to travel to Gurnee Mills, where we could get a hold of some exclusive fashion. Of course, we could have gone online to do the shopping, but we were young and wanted to be there in the physical. The mall still appealed to us more than the computer did, so that's what we did. We loaded into her Jeep and got onto I-94 on our way to Gurnee, Illinois, where the shopping district was crazy.

***

"I see you trying to do the most on me right now, girl. You better look at that price tag again," I said to Rosie as she marveled in front of the big mirror in a Ferragamo gown. They wanted $1,700 for that sucka, and then another $800 for the heels. This girl was tripping, and I almost left her ass in the store.

She kept holding the gown to her body, turning and looking over her shoulder at her rump, poking it in and out and licking her lips. "I'll have all them niggas at that party eating out the palm of my hand with this one. Damn, I look good, and I ain't even did my hair yet." She looked at the mirror head-on and hoisted up her breasts.

"Girl, unless you got some money to pay for that, you might as well throw that back onto the rack, because you done lost your damn mind if you think I'm about to spend all of my money on it for you just so you can outshine me at my own party." I rolled my eyes. "You got another thing coming, straight up."

She acted like I didn't even exist. She kept looking herself over until finally I walked away and into another aisle. I was down to spend some cake on her, but not half of my money. If I bought her that dress, it would mean I would have to wear something way cheaper. She would definitely be the center of attention, and I couldn't have that. After all, this was my day.

I snatched me up a nice body-hugging Prada mini dress with Elie Saab heels, and I took it upon myself to snatch her up the same fit, but in a different color, and her heels were an inch higher than mine. She was cool with that and kept on thanking me.

***

By the time we got back to her house, the sun was just

starting to go down. She let me use her shower and a few beauty products, and in her bathroom I made myself look like a chocolate angel. I stepped out of there looking like a billion dollars, if I do say so myself. I had curled my hair and had it hanging low over my shoulders. I felt it offset my outfit. I put on a little eyeliner and some lip gloss, and I was good to go.

Rosie came into her room and she wasn't even dressed yet. I was confused as to why that was because she had told me she was going to get dressed downstairs in her mother's bathroom. I could already hear the music being played loudly, and I figured the guests would be arriving any minute now.

She came in and kissed me on the cheek. "Damn, mami, you look real good. That Prada doing you justice, girl."

I smiled and ran my hands over my stomach. "Thank you, but why aren't you dressed yet?" I asked, looking her up and down, starting to get an attitude.

She blushed. "Yeah, I know, I know, but I had a little distraction come through. But I'm good now, so get out and go downstairs. There are already some guests here. I'm going to get dressed, and I'll be down in a minute." She was trying to push me out of the room.

"But wait, you know I don't mess with a lot of people like that. I don't know half the kids you invited to my party." I felt a little nervous at trying to be all friendly with people I did not regularly associate with. I didn't like feeling fake or forcing anything, and I was horrible at remembering names – that was the worst part.

Rosie kept on pushing until I wound up in the hallway, and she wound up slamming her bedroom door in my face. "You'll be okay. They ain't nothing but regular people. I'll be down in a minute, so vas, muchachita." I heard her laughing through the door, and I couldn't help but smile. She was crazy, and I loved her.

My dress was so tight it made it hard to walk down the stairs. I could barely separate my legs far enough. I looked good, I knew that, but there was definitely a price to pay. My heels had my feet hurting already, and I was still trying to remember how to properly walk in them.

When I got to the bottom of the landing, my right foot buckled, and I was glad nobody saw that because I would have been so embarrassed. The lights were already low, and the music was Dej Loaf. That was my girl. I loved everything she put out, so I got to nodding my head and walking toward the voices I overheard.

Rosie's mother was just coming out of the kitchen with a platter full of drinks, and there were about ten kids from school standing around, bouncing to the music in a cool-like fashion. When I stepped in there and they saw me, they all got to saying happy birthday and giving me hugs, which was cool, even though I didn't know a single one of them. I had seen the girls a few places at school, but we weren't cordial toward one another. These were definitely kids from Rosie's circle, and the boys weren't even worth mentioning. They were not my type.

The doorbell kept ringing and ringing, and more and more guests came until the whole house was full and jumping. All I could smell in the air was weed and cigarettes and all kinds of different perfumes.

I was cornered by two seniors who played on the basketball team, and they were not trying to let me go nowhere. We were in the kitchen, and they had tricked me into there, saying they wanted tap water. I should have known that was odd, but my gullible-ass led them into the kitchen, and they pushed me right into the pantry and started coming at me from every direction with that teenage game of theirs.

"I'm saying, Alexis, why haven't we ever gotten to know

each other the right way?" Trill asked, taking one of my curls and pulling on it.

I smacked his hand away. "Boy, stop before you mess up my hair, and then you gon' have to get it done, and I know you ain't holding like that," I said, dismissing his ass off the rip. He was about six feet, three inches tall, kind of cute, but had way too much confidence. I didn't care how good he was on the basketball court, it did not help me look fly. I needed a man with some money, a man who was going to pamper me. All of that boy-meets-girl stuff did not appeal to me.

"Damn, I guess she told you," Ronney said, holding his fist in front of his mouth. That was probably because his teeth were so jacked up that if he laughed regularly, he knew he wouldn't have a shot in the dark. I didn't have the slightest attraction to him. I didn't like a boy who didn't know how to dress. His clothing selections were all over the place.

"Oh, don't worry, you're about to get your turn, too, because I don't like you either. You ain't my type. He would be if he had it together, but even if you did, I'd still have to pass on you and wait for the next bus."

Trill got to holding his stomach laughing at that one, but I didn't see nothing funny. I was speaking my honest thoughts to them, and they thought it was a game. I tried to bump him out of the way, but I felt Ronney grab hold of my arm.

"Hold on, Alexis. I'm saying you ain't gotta like us. You can still spend some time with us, though. I mean, we did come all the way over here just to celebrate your party. Now, that has to count for something, don't it?"

I looked at him and then back over to Trill and raised an eyebrow. "Y'all gon' get a piece of cake, just like everybody else, and we gon' smack some ice cream on side of that, and that's the best I can do." I tried to scoot past again, but this time Trill stood in my way. "Boy, move." I pushed him in his chest, and he didn't budge.

"I'm saying, you done already dissed us, so we ain't got shit to lose. I been peeping you at school all semester, and you got one of the coldest bodies there. I been wanting to put my hands all over it." At saying this, he reached around my body and grabbed my booty.

I was about to push him up off me, but then I felt Ronney reach around and cup my breasts. He actually squeezed them and kissed me on the back of the neck. I felt a cool chill go down my spine, and for a second I was frozen in place. Trill kept fondling my booty, and then Ronney had the nerve to slide his hand into my top, where he felt up my breasts while he sucked on the back of my neck. I couldn't move. I wanted to stop them from doing what they were doing, but it was all feeling so damn good that I decided to roll with it. I knew what boundaries I wasn't willing to let them cross, and as long as they didn't, I was going to let them do them.

Ronney dropped to his knees, pushed my mini dress up my hips, and kissed me straight on my naked booty. I did have a thong on, but he didn't pay that no mind. I felt his lips on me, and it felt so good, especially when Trill leaned in and started sucking on my neck and kind of biting me with his teeth. I liked that shit so much I pulled him closer to me as I felt Ronney sliding his fingers past my thong.

That pantry was cramped, and every time I moved a certain way I was bumping into a bag of sugar or flour, but I didn't care. I wanted to feel them more. I don't know what came over me, but the moment they flipped that switch inside me, I just couldn't contain myself. I started moaning, and I helped Trill get my bra off while Ronney started sucking on my cheeks and licking in between them with his tongue.

I was standing there bow-legged with my ass poked out, and that's just how Rosie's mother found me. Her eyes damn near jumped from her face, especially when the boys shot past her and left me there to straighten my clothes. She didn't say nothing for a long time. Finally, she turned me around and helped to refasten my bra. I felt horrible.

"Baby, the house is full, and everybody is looking for the birthday girl, but here you are in the pantry, damn near in your birthday suit." She started laughing and shaking her head. "I ain't mad at you, though. To be young and wild, I miss that shit." She leaned in and kissed me on the cheek, then patted my rump. "G'on out there and enjoy yourself."

Even though I was feeling some type of way, that's exactly what I intended to do. I didn't know how I had managed to let them do that to me, but in that moment, it's like my body was calling out to them, and I could not deny their sexual energy. It was like I needed it. I needed to feel their hands on me, and I needed to feel their arousals because of me. I felt like I was cursed, and when it came down to sex, I could not deny my own urges. I was hot blooded and fiendin' for it all the time. All it took was the slightest touch and my jewel would perk up, ready for action. But the crazy part was I was still technically a virgin because I had not gone all the way with anyone. I'd played around some, but my flower was still intact.

Rosie's mom had activated the strobe light, and it flashed on and off, making me feel like I was moving in slow motion. The house was packed by this time, and as I made my way to the living room where everyone was dancing, I had to brush against a whole bunch of people on my way to find Rosie. I felt more than once a person grab my ass. It was pointless trying to see who it was because the place was so dark, and them damn lights were flashing on and off.

It took me a little while, but I should have known I would find her in the middle of the dance floor, twerking on this tall black dude who had his shirt off, grinding all on her ass. She had her hands on the floor, and he was all up in that booty. If they didn't have clothes on, she would have wound up pregnant. I stood there watching her as some li'l short boy tried to dance on me from behind. I turned around and pushed him away from me because I was not in the mood at that time. He looked all offended as he waved me off and said something I couldn't quite make out.

As the song ended, Rosie finally stood up, and the dude moved off of her ass. She turned around to face him and kissed him on the lips while he rubbed all over her ass, and that was when I noticed she had on the Ferragamo dress from earlier that we could not afford. Not only that, but she had on the heels that strapped all the way around her legs as well. I was trying to think back on a time when she could have had the opportunity to snatch them, but I remembered being with her the whole time. I couldn't help shaking my head because whenever Rosie wanted something, she always found a way to get it.

I walked out into the circle where she was hugged up with that dude and pulled her to the side. He was acting like he didn't want to let her go, and she was digging that shit. I could see it all in her face. "Damn, Rosie, leave that nigga alone for a minute so I can holler at you."

She laughed and threw her arm around my shoulder. I could smell the weed coming off of her skin. "Damn, sis, chill. Come on, let's go upstairs for a minute."

We pushed our way through the crowd, and once again I felt hands all over my ass. Obviously, she did, too, because she kept hollering out, "You're welcome," or, "That one's on the house," until we got to the stairs, which she tripped over twice before climbing them properly. I had to hold her up.

"Come on, Rosie. What the fuck is the matter with you?"

I asked, getting a little annoyed. We finally made it up to her room, where she flopped down on the bed on her back and left her legs wide open, so much so I could see she wasn't wearing panties with her new get-up. She took her fingers and ran them through her sex, and then rubbed her fingers together.

"I knew he had me wet. I'm glad you came and got me when you did, or else I was about to fuck him right on that dance floor, no bullshit." She closed her legs and sat up.

I closed her bedroom door and turned on the air conditioner because her room was kind of stuffy, then I sat down on the bed right next to her. "Who was that boy, anyway?" I asked, feeling curious.

She jumped up and turned around in a circle. "Bitch, he's the one that bought me this." She got to dancing a little bit, and I couldn't help laughing.

"Ain't that the same fit we passed up on in Gurnee?"

She nodded her head. "Hell yeah. You know I had to have it, and since my best friend acting all stank, I had to make other arrangements." She got down on her knees and dragged a bag from under the bed. "Boom! And that's yours, right there. You already know if a nigga tricking on me, then he gotta trick on you as well."

I looked like a kid on Christmas tearing open a present, I bussed that bag down so fast and opened the box. Inside was another Ferragamo fit, and inside of a smaller box was Alexander McQueen heels. My face lit up so fast, especially when I saw the receipt. He had dropped some coins on us.

I looked over at her and she was nodding her head with her eyes closed, laughing. "Did I do you right or did I do you right, girlfriend?" she slurred. She got up and sat on my lap on the bed. I wrapped my arms around her and kissed her cheek. She pressed her face harder into my lips, then she stood up and pulled up her gown, then sat back on my lap, straddling me. I

95

held her, feeling her weight on my legs. She laid her head on my shoulder, and we sat like that for a few minutes before somebody got to knocking on the door.

"Who is it?" she asked, not leaving my lap.

"Girl, you better come down here and tend to this company. How the hell y'all gon' be throwing a party when y'all up here in the room?" her mother yelled through the door.

"Okay, Mom, we'll be down in a minute."

"No, how about you make it a second? And those people called for Alexis. They said she is an hour past her curfew."

I winced at hearing that. I had not even had the chance to fully enjoy my party yet, and they were wanting me home like they were missing me or something.

I tried to stand up, and Rosie got the hint. "I guess we better go downstairs and finish the party," I said, hugging her. She melted into my arms and agreed.

It must have been the liquor, or maybe it was the weed, because when I went to let her go, she pulled my chin downward and we started making out right there, standing up, with her hands squeezing my ass. I felt awkward at first, but then that switch flipped and I backed her all the way up to the bed until we fell on it with me between her legs, which wrapped around me. Somehow my dress had ridden up until it was beyond my stomach, and hers had peeled away as well, because I felt her hot pussy scalding my abdomen with its prickly hairs. She was as wet as advertised, and I couldn't stop myself from running my fingers between her lips. This drove her crazy and made her hump upward toward my hand while she sucked on my neck. I could smell her essence in the air, and that excited me all the more.

I scooted down her body, turned her around to her stomach, and spread her cheeks. I took my tongue and dragged it all up and down her crease until her jewel popped out. I trapped that with my lips and sucked on it until she screamed at the top of her lungs.

This was my best friend and we had never done anything like that before, but it didn't feel weird at all. It felt necessary, and I was craving her body just as much as she was mine. I guess secretly I had always lusted after her. It was more of a subconscious thing. I think all girls find their friends attractive, and if given the opportunity to play, they would. Well that's where I was. I would, and I was, and it felt right.

I spread her legs further apart and worked my fingers into her kitten three at a time while I sucked on her neck up top. As soon as she started humping the bed, I turned into a maniac, and my fingers took on a mind of their own. I drove them into her so fast they became a blur. She laid her head on the bed with saliva coming from her open mouth. Her moans, if even a slight bit louder, would give us away, but that did not make me bring down the intensity.

When she came up onto her knees, it gave me more access, and I took full advantage. I grabbed her long hair, making her arch her back, and I ran four fingers into her while she bounced back into them with tears in her eyes.

***

We finally made it downstairs, and the party was still jumping as if we had never left. As soon as Rosie stepped off the last stair, the dark-skinned dude from earlier was all up in her grill. She started laughing and flirting, then took the time to introduce us.

"Alexis, this is li'l Chris. And li'l Chris, this is Alexis."

He walked toward me with his arms open and I let him hug me. "So, this the birthday girl, then, huh?"

"Yeah. It's nice to meet you, and thank you for the gift.

You didn't have to go all-out like that."

He smiled, and for the first time I was able to see he had a mouth full of gold. I found that attractive.

"Like they say, it ain't tricking if you got it, and I definitely got it to trick."

I nodded my head and sized him up. I had never seen him at school before, and even if I did, I don't know if I would have been feeling him just off his looks. It was kind of dark, so I couldn't peep his attire, but I did see he had a fat-ass gold watch on his wrist and a few chains around his neck. He looked like money, and that got me wet, I ain't gon' even lie.

"So, where are your guys at? Don't tell me you're the only one of your crew that's winning?"

Rosie stepped in between us and backed her ass up on him. He leaned down and kissed her on the neck. "Nall, I only fuck with one other dude, and he on his way over here right now. It's my homey, but we're more like brothers than anything else. He just put a line through his broad, too, and turned her into an X, so I think y'all should meet because he loves dark-skinned females with first-class bodies."

Rosie interrupted him. "Damn. I'm saying what about me?"

He kissed her again and pulled her back into him. "Aw, I'm saying you definitely not flying coach. Your shit tight, too. That's why I keep you with bands and working the latest. Long as that pussy tight, I got you."

I was digging this nigga, and I would have fucked him right there in front of Rosie. Any dude that carried his self with that much confidence and had the dollars to back it up was like a god to me. I was trying to work on a proposal in my head for Rosie to get her to see why we should be sharing him.

"So, how long before your guy gets here?" I really didn't care, but I wanted to keep the conversation going. The disco light was shining off of his gold, and I was getting turned on by that. I even felt my juice running down my leg.

He straightened up the Tom Ford glasses on his nose and looked down to his gold watch, using the light from his phone to illuminate it. "He should be on his way right now. He had to make some drop-offs down in the Ada B. Wells on 39ᵗʰ, and that was about thirty minutes ago. Don't worry, I'm gon' put you in, though. I got you."

I wasn't thinking about his homey, I wanted his ass. I would have let him do anything to me, too. I was trying to factor in my love for Rosie, and I had to really ask myself if I would fuck this nigga behind her back. The way I was feeling in that moment, I probably would have. I'd confess to her later, but I'd definitely have to see what his sex game was like.

T.J. & Jelissa

Chapter 10

Alexis

I forgot all about my party going on inside. I was too mesmerized by li'l Chris. I was hanging onto every word he was saying and praying that he didn't stop talking. Every word that formed into a sentence, then turned into a paragraph made me pant for him. He was doing some first-class jacking, and I was loving every minute of it.

I was standing so close to him I could smell his cologne, and that smelled expensive. When we got onto the porch, I was finally able to really see him and what he had on, and if I had been spent before, I was even more so now. He was dressed in a blue and black Dolce & Gabbana fit with the Ferragamo shoes and belt to match. He was rocking a Rolex, and the two diamonds in his earlobes were causing me to choose him even harder.

Rosie could tell I was feeling her man, too, because she kept on giving me the evil eye while he held her. I was so caught up in how I was feeling that I didn't even pay that shit no attention.

I didn't think anything could get me to take my mind off of him until his guy pulled up in an all-black Porsche 911GT3 with the red ground effects and lights on the bottom of it. The shoes on his whip were also black and red, and he hopped out fitted in a Gucci fit that matched his car. He was light skinned, looked to be mixed with Asian, but he had this curly hair and slanted eyes that were gray. He walked up to us on the porch, and I was stuck. I had never seen a dude as fine as him.

He gave li'l Chris a hug while Rosie and I stood to the side, drinking him in.

"Yo, Rosie and Alexis, this is my mans, Prince. Prince,

this right here is Rosie, my boo thang, and that chocolate specimen over there is Alexis. She the one I was telling you about that you had to meet."

I started blushing off the rip. I put my head down and tried to make myself as small as I could, but that didn't stop him from walking up to me and opening his arms. "I'm saying, Ms. Hershey, what's it gon' take for me to get a hug from you?"

I could smell his cologne, and it drove my senses haywire. I was feeling shy as hell, and I didn't know what to do with myself. I slowly walked into his arms until he wrapped them around me and held me close. I could feel his muscles, and I felt so small in that moment. Finally, I wrapped my arms around him as well, and we stayed like that for a few seconds before it started to feel weird.

"That's what I'm talking about," Rosie said, snuggling up to her man. "Y'all look real nice together. That yellow-on-black shit always look good mixed, don't it babe?" she said, looking up at Li'l Chris.

He scooped her up into the air, and she yelped before wrapping her legs around him and flashing us her bare ass. "You already know this," he said.

Prince took a step back and looked me up and down. "I'm saying, how can I get to know you a little better? Can we go down and sit in my whip?"

I took one last look back at my party going on inside before following him down to his Porsche.

Inside it looked like a space ship. He had a lot going on, and there were so many digital screens everywhere I didn't know how he didn't get confused. When we were standing outside of his car, I couldn't hear any music, but as soon as he opened the door it was blaring loud as ever. I had to cover my ears from the sound of the Forever We Shine music. I mean, I loved the song, it was just too damn loud. He grabbed the big digital remote and lowered it until you could barely hear Caliph and Gotto slicing the track up.

I slid into his leather seat, and it immediately started to massage my rump. It felt good, and so did the cool air coming from the vents. When he slid into the driver's seat and closed the door, I got all shy again. The song switched over to one by Brittany White, and the mood felt so magical. I didn't say nothing for a long time, and neither did he.

"So, tell me, Alexis, what do you want for your birthday?" he asked, and I still was afraid to look over at him. Finally, I did, and I noted he was taking a big automatic off of his lap and pushing it under his seat until all that could be seen was the handle.

I shrugged my shoulder. "I don't know. I mean, my party was nice. I don't think I can ask for any more than that."

He laughed out loud. "Man, baby, stop playing with me. You see all this?" He pulled out a knot of money from his arm rest and sat it on his lap. It looked like it was all $100 bills. "Now, you can have whatever you like. It's your day. All you have to do is tell me what's good."

I was stuck there looking like a fool. I had never been stunted on before, and I didn't know if he was just jacking on me or if he was serious. I didn't want to come off like a gold digger or a groupie, so I tried to maintain my composure. "All the stores are closed already, so even if I had something in mind, you wouldn't be able to go and get it for me at this hour."

He rubbed his chin and looked as if he were in deep thought. "Yeah, I guess you are right. Damn, I didn't think about all that, huh."

We sat silent again, and the track switched over on the radio. Outside I could see the party starting to let out. Rosie stood between her man's legs while he sat on the hood of his own Porsche, and it looked identical to the one I was sitting in, if not for the color, which was all gray with black guts.

"And besides, you don't have to get me anything anyway. We just met. What type of chick would that make me if I was expecting something from you already?"

He kept on rubbing his chin as if he had a whole bunch of hair there, which there wasn't. "Alight, then, so what are the odds of me getting to know you?"

I turned toward him. "That all depends on if you really want to. I already know there's plenty females jocking you because of the car you're driving, but that doesn't impress me," I lied, praying he wouldn't see through me.

He ran his hand over his waves and lowered his head. "Damn, I ain't never heard a female come at me like that before."

Just as he said that, I saw the Taylors' station wagon pull up in front of the house. I knew it was going to be trouble. I acted as if I didn't even see them. "Hey, Prince, those are my people right there, and I ain't trying to be fucking with them in this moment, so why don't you pull off before they get to raising hell."

He perked up in his seat and started the ignition. "Say no more."

The engine purred to life so quiet I could not even tell that it was on after the initial start of it. He coasted away from the curb after blowing his horn once to let Rosie and Lil Chris know we were pulling away. They followed suit, and less than ten seconds later we all stopped at the red lights on Halstead, where he rolled down the window on my side.

Lil Chris dropped his top, and then I felt Prince's coming off as well.

"Yo, where you trying to go, bro? I'm hungry as hell, and I know my li'l chocolate princess trying to eat something, ain't you?" he asked me. I nodded.

"Yo, let's hit up Gwen's Soul Food joint out in the Wild 100s. You with that?" Li'l Chris yelled from his ride.

I saw Rosie's head go down in his lap, and I couldn't do nothing but act like I didn't notice what she was doing.

"Yeah, that's bet! Princess, you got a taste for some real good soul food?" he asked me.

I didn't know if I was feeling him calling me Princess, but I kept looking down at all of that money in his lap and just rolled with it. "Yeah, I could eat."

Prince revved his engine, and Li'l Chris did the same thing. The next thing I knew we were hitting speeds of 130 while I tried my best to pull my seatbelt across my chest. My eyes were open so wide I couldn't even blink. That fool was speeding past cars and weaving through the traffic. I was scared as hell. I felt like I was on a roller coaster ride that could actually kill me.

I damn near threw up all over my window when he drove onto the sidewalk just to scare this bum half to death. The old man was standing in front of his shopping cart with a bottle of wine pressed to his lips. His instincts must have told him that danger was approaching, because as soon as he managed to look up, that's when Prince hopped the curb and started to drive directly at him.

I was so scared I couldn't even close my eyes. My heart got to beating in my chest like it was swinging a sledgehammer. I was trying to escape my seat the closer we got to him, but the reality was I didn't have anywhere to go, so I pressed my back into my seat and held my breath as the bum's body was coming up fast in front of us.

"Oh my god, oh my god, oh my god! Prince, what are you doing?" I screamed through a cracking voice.

"Yeah, I'm about to run his ass down! Yeah, muthafucka!"

he said as he stepped on the accelerator.

I don't know how I managed to keep my food inside of me. Maybe it was the fact I didn't have anything inside of me because I had not eaten that whole day, or maybe I was just too afraid to puke. Either way, I had never been that scared in my life, and as I saw that man's body coming closer and closer, I almost fainted.

Luckily, at the last minute, Prince swerved and jumped back onto the street. I had closed my eyes at this time, and when I opened them I looked into my rear-view mirror and saw the bum was in the middle of the street, trying to throw rocks at the car. I was just glad that he was still alive.

I was so pissed I punched Prince straight in the arm. "What the fuck is your problem, dude?"

"Ah, shit, shorty, chill. I was just having a little fun. I wasn't gon' hit that old nigga. Besides, dude done fucked over a lot of people in his life. If you only knew, you'd probably let me hit his ass."

Just as we were flying through the intersection, Lil Chris's car came into view. This fool had the nerve to stop and burn a 360 in the middle of the street. His tires were spinning so fast smoke started to come from them.

Prince, not to be outdone, started to do the same thing. I really didn't have no problem with this; it was kind of cool.

The traffic had stopped around us, and we were the center of attention. I looked over and into Li'l Chris's car and saw Rosie's head moving up and down still. By the time we scurried away, there were two police cars flying down the street directly toward us.

Now, I was getting a little spooked, especially when Prince hit a U-turn and headed directly for them. Li'l Chris did the same thing, so we wound up passing the cars and they had to turn around to get behind us.

Well, by this time we were flying down an alley, and Prince had turned his music all the way up. I felt like I was in a movie watching him maneuver his car. That shit had me scared and turned on at the same time.

I reached over and grabbed his dick and squeezed it. He stuck his tongue out, so I reached down and unbuckled his pants and popped his man out. I felt like Rosie couldn't be the only one with a crazy-ass baller. I had to step my game up, so I stuck my hand under my dress to play in my goodies while I licked around his helmet before popping it in my mouth. It felt hot and tasted salty, but I was so turned on I just got to doing what I was supposed to, like a pro.

I could hear the sirens somewhere behind us, but I could tell he had lost them for the most part. He kept on making sharp turns that were causing his piece to go further down my throat than I liked, but I rolled with it. Before I knew it he was spitting up, catching me off guard.

***

We pulled into the empty Navy Pier yard five minutes before Rosie and Li'l Chris showed up. By that time, I had my legs wide open while Prince feasted on my goodies. He had my seat leaned all the way back with my legs on his shoulders, eating me like he was trying to pay a debt. The sounds I was making were so crazy that afterward I was embarrassed. I just could not believe I had this fine dude between my legs, eating me for all I was worth. His fingers ran in and out of me and were driving me up the wall, and when I finally started to shake, I screamed for him to suck harder on my jewel. And he did, too.

***

When we finished, he sucked his fingers and told me I had a sweet kitty cat. I was so embarrassed by the sounds I had made that I couldn't even look him in the face. All I could do was smile and keep my head lowered.

Lil Chris stepped out of his car, walked over to Prince's, and handed him a blunt so fat it looked like a mini carpet rolled up. Prince took his lighter and put fire to it while Rosie came over and hugged my neck. I got out of the car and we walked along the beach, holding hands. I could smell sex all on her, and to my surprise it didn't bother me at all.

"Aw, so y'all gon' leave us in the parking lot, huh?" Prince yelled, holding his arms up in the air.

We both started laughing. I looked back and held up one finger to them. I just needed to holler at my girl for a minute. "So, what's good with these niggaz? Why you ain't been put me up on them?"

She started laughing and then wiped her mouth with her hand, acting like she was spitting something out. She stuck out her tongue and pulled what seemed to be a hair off of it. I knew that's what it was because she held it up to her eye and I saw it was curly.

"See, that's what I'm saying, mami. These niggaz gotta start trimming they shit, because I ain't about to be swallowing no niggaz kids and his pubic hairs, too. They always talking about they like a bald pussy. Well, shit, the feeling is mutual on our end, too. What makes them think we like all that hair and shit? Ugh!" She curled up the side of her lip and shook her head.

I did have to agree with her on that one. I didn't have that much experience when it came to men, but I knew off the rip that I wouldn't like a whole lot of hair down there while I was performing. "Don't try and change the subject. I said, why you ain't been put me up on game when it came to them?"

She smiled again, still picking on her tongue. After ensuring she was good to go, she stuck it back into her mouth, rolled it around, and spit into the grass, then wiped her lips and popped a piece of gum in.

"I don't know, sis. I guess I was gon' try and fuck with both of them niggaz, because they fine in two different ways. Plus they are in their own lanes, and I like that shit. They having that stupid cash, and you know who their fathers are, right?"

I was completely oblivious and stuck on the fact she said she was going to try and fuck with the both of them. I had to applaud her courage. She was definitely secure in who she was as a person. "Nall, who are they?" I asked, trying to regain my train of thought.

"Yo, you must have been sleeping under a rock. That's King and Chris's sons. You know them dudes from the Young Radicals? They were the ones that forced all of them people to take that pure laboratory-produced heroin all throughout the projects in Chicago and Indiana. I mean, they made so much money in the span of five years that they were able to buy into the Bulls and Bears franchises. Now, they're filthy rich. Prince's dad just got back out of prison, and Li'l Chris's dad owns all of those strip clubs from here to Atlanta. They call them the Dope Game Geniuses because of how they did things and the way they got rich so fast." She paused to look over at them. They were whipping and nae-nae-ing in the parking lot, dancing like fools with big blunts burning in their fingers. "Yeah, them niggaz sitting on millions, and I'm definitely trying to get up under one of them. But since you my girl, I'm gon' let you do your thing, too."

I kept sizing them up. I could not believe what I was hearing. I had never been around a millionaire before, and I was starting to turn shell-shocked. What was I supposed to do now? I was getting all shy again. "So, what do I do?"

Her eyes lowered, and she curled up her mouth. "All men are alike. All you have to do is play on their physical weaknesses and mentally fuck them before they can do it to you. Everything is about mental manipulation, but you have to be the first on the draw. You have to be the smart one, but act as if you aren't. Make it seem like they have the lead when really they are following your every scheme. Play to win, and live in the moment. Get it while the getting is good, because niggaz like them get bored easily. Your goal should be to have one of their babies, that way you can trap them. I know that's what I'm on. I been sticking holes in me and Li'l Chris's condoms for two weeks now, plus I just sucked his dick so good he let me bounce up and down on it in the raw. I made sure he skeeted deep in me, too. I even held my own kitty lips together, making sure didn't none of that shit drip out. Shit, I gotta get mines."

She kept looking at them as if she hated them. Her eyes were far away, yet she seemed so focused.

I nodded. "Yeah, I hear you, girl. I definitely hear you."

"Damn! I'm saying, we finna go and get something to eat, or what?" Prince yelled.

***

We rolled out and wound up at Gwen's Soul Food joint. We all must have been hungry, because all I could hear was smacking and the sucking of fingers. I kept it gangsta and ate like I ain't have no home training. I didn't even realize how hungry I was until I saw all of them chowing down. Rosie was feeding her man and stuffing food into her own mouth at the same time. She even burped twice and kept on eating after punching herself in the chest and drinking from her lemonade.

Li'l Chris was smacking so loud and talking with his mouth full. "You see, that's why this my baby, right here, because she keep shit all the way gangsta. I don't give a fuck what I got going on in my life, I'm gon' make sure she straight."

He leaned over and kissed her, and Rosie winked her eye at me. I was jealous as hell because she had her game on point. I had to step mine up.

I saw Prince had some barbeque sauce on his face, so I took my napkin and wiped it for him. "Baby, you're too fine to be looking all out of place. Let mommy get that for you." After I finished wiping it away, I kissed him on the cheek. He perked up and smiled, then I put his lemonade to his lips for him to drink. "Here you go, baby."

He accepted my show of affection and sipped from his cup. "Oh, I see you trying to boo me up, huh? Well, I gotta be honest, I'm feeling this with your li'l chocolate ass."

The restaurant was a small establishment, but the food was off the chain. The interior was cozy and the lights were dimmed. It made a person feel very comfortable. Gwen walked over to our table in her apron. "Can I get you angels anything else, or would that be all for the night?"

Prince got to sucking on his fingers all loud and dried them on a napkin. He reached into his pocket and pulled out a big knot of money and handed it to her. "This should be enough right here, grandma," he said, smiling at her with his handsome face. "And where is my kiss at?"

She took all of the bills and put them into her bra. "Boy, now you know I don't accept no drug money in here. I only take righteous, hard-earned paper. I mean, what kind of woman would that make me if—"

She busted out laughing, and so did he. I mean, she bent

over. cackling at the top of her lungs. She was laughing so hard she made me start laughing.

"Y'all almost believed me, huh? Look at this one's face right here. She was feelin' all sad for me and stuff. Sugar, it's gon' be okay. I'm from the old school, baby. I don't care if these bills had blood on them. Somebody die every day. Should I feel bad because the money they was supposed to spend wound up in my pocket? You can't take it to Heaven with you, and you know why that is, don't you?" she asked, looking right at me.

I shook my head.

"That's because God ain't about to let them white folks' face appear on nothing of value up there." She pointed toward the sky. "They got it all down here already. We have to work so damn hard to make ends meet, so I accept drug money, blood money, Crip money, and ho money, too. It all spends the same, and that's the only way I'm gon' be able to call myself a... what is it, grandson?"

Li'l Chris laughed. "A boss, ma."

"Yeah, a boss."

He pulled out another knot and handed it to her. "And this is your tip and for you being you. You know we love you." He got up and gave her a kiss.

I don't know what it was, but I liked the dark-skinned older lady. I liked her curly hair and her personality. I thought she must have felt lucky to have known them if they were always cashing her out like that.

***

"So, I'm saying, when am I gon' see you again, Princess?"

We were sitting in front of the Taylors' house, and I was

so afraid to go in there. The sun was starting to peek over the horizon, and I knew it was going to be hell to pay the captain. I couldn't even think of an excuse good enough for staying out for as long as I did. I simply shrugged my shoulders.

I turned back to Prince. "I like you, Prince, but it don't have anything to do with your money. I need you to know that off the rip. I know you probably getting sweated because of who your father is, but I feel like a real man can create his own legacy and not live in the shadows of the ones before him. You have to stand out and find your own limelight. I think you are a nice person, and I got a little carried away with the head situation, but I have no regrets. If you want to see me again, you'll find a way."

I leaned over and kissed him on the cheek, then took my purse from between his legs, not even taking the time out to think about how it got there.

I took a deep breath and tried to prepare myself for what was to come. I didn't care what they were about to do as long as they didn't try and put their hands on me. I wasn't going for that.

T.J. & Jelissa

Chapter 11

Tiny

After all of the waiting and hassling, I was finally given my interview with the warden. I was sitting outside of his office across from his secretary, nervous as hell. I didn't know what to do or what to think. I needed this job more than any job of my life. I had to get out of this prison and make it home to my daughter before she got too far gone. I couldn't help praying out loud. "Lord, please, you know what kind of bind I am in. You know I did not kill that woman, and I have been in here for way too long. I beg of you to have mercy on my soul. Please allow me to land this job, please help this job get me out of these gates and home to my daughter, where I belong. Forgive me for my iniquities. I pray these things and all things through the vessel of Jesus. Amen." I kept on bouncing my leg up and down on one foot and could not contain myself.

When his secretary's phone rang, I had a feeling they were talking about me. She sat in her chair with the phone to her old ear, looking at me as if I didn't know what was up. I didn't like her for some reason. Maybe it was her curly white wig that was throwing me off, or maybe it was the fact when I first came in, instead of her greeting me as a professional, she just pointed to the chair I was supposed to sit in. That annoyed me to a fault.

She hung up the phone and pointed to the door behind her. "You may go in now, Ms. Johnson. He's waiting for you."

I squinted my eyes at her and smiled all fake-like. I ain't like her, and that was that. I took a deep breath and knocked on the door.

"Come on in, Ms. Johnson," I heard him say.

I twisted the knob and took one more deep breath before

stepping inside his big office. He had his ear to a phone and directed me to sit in front of his desk. He mouthed the word *sorry* to me and turned a picture around on his desk of what had to be his wife. Then he did the talking sign with his hands to indicate she was running her mouth a mile a minute on the other end. I smiled at that. At least he had a sense of humor. He was attractive, too, for an older white man. He still had all of his hair, and it was as neat as George Clooney's. In fact, he favored him somewhat.

I saw a bucket of cleaning supplies in the corner of his office, and I got right up and grabbed them and started doing my thing. I wasn't about to wait for him to interview me; I was going to get myself hired. Fuck that. This was a mission I could not fail.

I started by dusting his blinds and cleaning the windows. Then I worked my way on back toward him, sanitizing everything in my path. I even lifted the stuff off of his desk and cleaned it. All the while his wife had his ear on the phone, and he didn't stop me or say a word. I got down on my knees and made sure my ass was in the air facing him as I cleaned under his desk and around it. When I had to lean down facing him, I made sure he could see down my top. I kept pinching my nipples when he couldn't see me to keep them hard. I was going all out, and I was down to do anything to get home to my baby.

Finally, he hung up the phone and asked me to sit down. By that time all I had left to do was vacuum his rug. I sat down reluctantly, praying he was still in a good mood. I crossed my legs and ran my tongue across my lips. I knew if a white man liked a sistah, it was because of her body. And they were crazy about our lips, so I kept mine shiny with spit for him.

"So, Ms. Johnson, you want to work for me, do you?" he asked, opening up my file. "Wow, a murderer. Should I be worried?"

I fidgeted nervously in my seat. I was so tired of everybody calling me that. I had never killed anyone, and I felt like Lisa's death would always haunt me. I wanted to tell him I wasn't a murderer, and I was innocent, and all I wanted to do was get home to my daughter, but for some reason all of my energy just left my body, and all I could do was shake my head. "No, sir, you have no reason to be worried about me. But yes, I would love to work for you. It would be an honor."

He sat back and rocked in his chair. "I see. Well, what makes you think you deserve to be home earlier than what they sentenced you to? What makes you so damn special?"

Did he just curse at me? I know I had to be hearing things. "Well, sir, since I have been down, I have been working really hard and staying out of trouble. I keep my nose clean, and I stay to myself. I really need to get home to my daughter as soon as I can because she is growing up in a cold, cold world. I know what it's like to not have anybody to depend on. It gets real lonely, and it makes it hard not to give up. I am willing to do anything to get this job and maintain it so I can get your recommendation for an early release to the community. I understand you are very powerful, and your influence means a lot to me."

His secretary knocked on the door and came in and handed him a steaming cup of coffee, which he sipped out of before placing it before him. "Well, I hear everything you are saying, but why should I give a fuck? Why should I care about some black chick that needs my recommendation? Screw you. So, what do you have to say about that?"

Now I was getting irritated. This white dude had me fucked all the way up. I know he wasn't sitting there acting like he was God, talking about why should he care and calling me a black chick. That was starting to get me heated, but I had to play it cool. "Sir, with all due respect, I don't like how you're coming at me."

He shrugged his shoulders. "So what? What are you going to do about it?" he asked as if he were challenging me.

I felt my blood starting to boil. It was taking all of the patience I had inside of me to not snap out and attack his ass. I couldn't even look up at him because I knew me, and I knew I was seconds away from being all over his ass.

"Come on, Zivial, let me see that black passion. Show me how angry you can get. I want to see the fire in your belly. Turn me on."

His eyes lowered, and I couldn't see what he was doing behind his desk, but something told me something wasn't right. I took a gamble and decided to play into his fantasy. "Mr. Towers, you will not like me if I get mad. You never want to see a black woman mad, I'm telling you this."

He closed his eyes. "Yeah, whatever. I don't believe you. I think you are bluffing. Show me. Show me what happens when a black woman gets angry. I need to see it." His voice became raspy, and he refused to open his eyes to look at me.

I got up and locked the door, then I stood over him and looked into his face before tilting his chin upward. "Listen here, white man, this ain't my first rodeo. Now, I know what you expect out of me, and I am willing to give it to you if that means you are going to help me get back out into the community. I'll be your slave, daddy, and I'll do everything you want me to do. I'll suck your dick so good you'll forget all about your wife and your problems at home. It can be all about us, baby. I'll be your Brown Sugar Momma." I dropped down to my knees and started to loosen his belt.

He moaned and opened his legs as wide as he could as I slid his pants down his legs. The man was so perverted he didn't even have on underwear. His little pink dick sprung up the size of my pinkie. I almost wanted to laugh at him, but I had to remember what was at stake. "Damn, daddy, you got all of this meat for your black baby? What do you want me to do with it?"

He laid his head back on his chair and groaned. "Suck me, baby. Suck me into your black mouth until I cream in your coffee."

I had to laugh at that little metaphor. I opened my lips and sucked him in and twirled my tongue around his helmet until he was squirming in his seat. I mean, my head disappeared in his lap again and again. I was trying to win the job the old-fashioned way, and I could tell it was going to be mine by the way he was humping up out of his chair with tears rolling down his cheeks.

"You like that, daddy? Am I doing you right?" I said between loud sucks. He had the nerve to reach out and grab hold of my head. I usually didn't like this, but I was no stranger to being a ho. I knew every trick was different, and each one had their thing or their go-to way of coming. I felt that since he was grabbing onto my head, he was almost there, so I sucked harder and nipped his head with my teeth a little.

"Oh, Sugar Momma, you're driving me nuts! You're driving me crazy, baby! Here it comes. Oh my god, here it comes!"

For such a little dick, he sprayed me as if he was packing a hose. I tried my best to keep playing along, but it became too much of a burden to swallow, so it started spilling down my neck. I think that drove him crazy, because he fell to the floor and started kissing my feet over and over. The only thing that kept going through my head was *book it!*

***

The next morning, I woke up with a pep in my step because they had slid a paper under my door telling me I was assigned to work in the warden's wing starting the following Monday. I was so happy I couldn't even eat. I didn't even want to leave my room for fear I would go out into the population and get into it with another female, making them throw me in the hole, and before I even started my job, I would have lost it. I felt like I had that kind of luck, so I didn't want to gamble with it. I felt blessed, and I didn't want anything to ruin that.

One thing about the females in prison was once they found out you were onto something positive, they always tried to find a way to knock you off your square. It was a dog-eat-dog world, and I was tired of going through it, I was ready to be free and out and about, living life. I was tired of the bars and the chains. I was tired of showering with twenty other women and worrying about if I was going to be shanked or not. I was tired of the food and the roaches that came along with the platters. I just wanted to be done with it all.

I sat there in my room on my bunk, wallowing in my iniquities, thinking about my daughter and wondering what was going on with her. Every second we were apart it worried me because I knew how Chicago was: here today and gone tomorrow. It was a city of no remorse. I started to imagine some pretty graphic things, and my stomach was turning itself inside out. I was just about to head to the bathroom when the guard knocked on my door and told me I had a visit. Shock was written across my face. I was so happy I started stripping before she even left. I was anxious to get down there to see who it was, although I was banking on it being Roman.

So, imagine my face when I got into the visiting center and was met by a familiar face I had not seen in a long time. As soon as I came through the door and she saw me, she ran to me at full speed and wrapped her arms around.

"Momma! Oh my god, I have missed you so much!" Arianna cried into my chest.

I could not believe it was her. I had not seen her since she was about six years old when her foster parents stop bringing her to see me.

Arianna was the daughter of one of my best friends, Amber, who had taken her own life after she'd gotten hooked on heroin. She was born prematurely and had gone through so many trials before she was even a week old. Now she stood before me, just as beautiful as any model. Her skin was the color of bronze and her body had filled out to that of a black woman, though her mother was white, making her fifty percent black. Her father was a man I was familiar with. He had been my pimp and had even gotten me pregnant before, but I had not made it that far along before he beat the baby out of me. Jaheim was his name, and I had never hated anyone as much as I did him.

Arianna held me tighter and cried harder into me. "Mom, I need you so bad. I just had to see you. I am so afraid of this world, and now that I am 18, my foster parents have pushed me out into the world and cut all ties with me. They said since they aren't getting paid for me anymore, they don't want anything to do with me. What am I to do?"

I patted her on the back. I was still in shock. I had forgotten her birthday was two days after my own daughter's, and they were a year apart. So, that's why she was up here by herself, because she had turned 18 and was officially an adult.

"Baby, why don't we sit down and you can tell me what's going on."

She nodded and let go of me reluctantly. We sat down across from each other.

"So, tell me everything."

She wiped her tears away and took a deep breath while

biting into her bottom lip. "Well, ever since I'd been living with them, they have done nothing but treat me wrong. I don't know why because I always try and do everything they tell me to do, but it's never good enough, and they are never satisfied with me. I can remember so many times breaking down, and cutting on my arm to dull the pains from them. I just wanted to be loved and accepted, but I never have been." She wiped her nose with the sleeve of her tight sweater. "Mrs. Jones, she has always hated me, and she never talks to me, or even looks at me without frowning up her face. And their daughter was cool with me until her boyfriend tried to hit on me and I told her about it. After that she kept on saying I thought I was better than her, and I never have. So we just never got along after that, and she started spreading these nasty rumors in school about me, that I was a slut and I would sleep with any guy at any time. Well, a whole bunch of guys started to see if that were the case. They started running all of this game on me, Mom, and I fell for their antics. I did some horrible things to a lot of boys."

She lowered her face into her lap and started bawling her eyes out. I reached over and rubbed her on the back.

"Baby, don't worry about that right now. Just continue so I can know everything, okay?"

A guard must have seen her crying because he came over and handed her a box of tissues. I thanked him before he nodded and walked off.

She blew so much snot out at one time that it wound up on her hand and dripped off of her wrist. I had to turn my head away or I was about to puke everywhere. She stood up, holding more tissue to her face, and went to the bathroom. After she got back, I could tell she had washed her face a little bit.

"I'm sorry, Mom. Where was I?" she asked, sitting down

so fast her chair squeaked.

"The part after the boys, baby." I looked into her face and she turned red and started blushing.

"Oh, yeah. Well. Anyway, I experimented a whole lot, and to be honest, it did make me feel a little better while I was doing the acts. But as soon as they were over, I would feel like crap until another guy was on top of me. This went on for a whole semester until my principal found out and wanted in on the action, to which I relented. That went on for a few months until he got jealous because I was found behind the bleachers with another senior boy by a teacher. So, in short, he ended things between us and even suspended me. Once Mr. Jones found out I was promiscuous, he started coming into my room at night and touching me. At first I was scared, but then he got to saying all the right things and telling me how much he cared about me, and how he would protect me. Well, before you knew it, we were sleeping together three times a day, in his car, in the basement, and even in his marital bed. He used to make me dress up like a school girl before he ravished me." She shook her head from side to side.

I was at a loss for words. I mean, damn, she almost had me beat. I didn't know what to say. I was afraid to look at her because I thought she would be able to see what I was thinking, and even I didn't know what that was.

"Mom, do you hate me so far?" she whimpered.

I reached across the table and rubbed her hand. "Baby, of course not. Go on, get everything out."

She bit into her bottom lip. "Okay, well, everything was cool between him and I for a little while. He started taking me out and buying me clothes – you know, treating me like a princess. You know, with the exception of the screwing me part. But he made me feel so good all the time. That was until his wife caught us in bed together." She shook her head.

"Everything went downhill after that."

I could only imagine what the wife did. Had I caught some li'l young, fine-ass girl in the bed with my husband, I would have killed them both and did my time with a smile on my face. It was a blessing she was here to tell her story. "Babe, what happened after that?"

She covered her face with both hands and started to bawl all over again. "She beat me every single night with a plastic bat all across my back. Then she would switch to a belt, and that would lead to her fists. I don't know how many times she knocked me out, but I know it's way too many to count." She broke down after that, and I wound up holding her in my arms for an entire hour while she cried.

I felt like my heart was separating into two. I could only imagine what she had been through. I was trying to muster up the words to help her get past her tragedy, but none were coming to me, which was odd. "Baby, where are you staying right now?"

She shook her head. "Nowhere, Mom. I have literally been sleeping on the streets."

"Well, don't worry. I'll take care of everything."

Chapter 12

Alexis

Before I could even put my key into the front door, it flew open, and Mrs. Taylor had the nerve to snatch me inside as if I were one of her kids. I already had a hard time walking in heels, so when she pulled me inside, I tripped all over my feet and fell flat on my face. My chin hit the floor and made me bite my tongue. I struggled to get up.

She slammed the door behind her. "Little girl, have you lost your muthafucking mind? How dare you bring your little black ass into this house at the same time the sun is coming up? Now, explain yourself! Right now," she demanded, standing over me.

Her breath sailed down to my face. It smelled as if she had gargled shitty water from the toilet just so she could come and talk to me with that shit on her breath. I was already mad because I was tasting blood in my mouth from my fall, and now I had this chubby standing over me like she was God or something.

I kicked them heels off of my feet and stood up to face her, trying my best to hold my breath because hers was kicking like a baby in a woman's stomach. "Mrs. Taylor, I get that you're upset with me right now, but don't you ever put your hands on me again. I'm not the one for that, okay?" I looked everywhere but into her eyes because I knew if I did, they would seem challenging, and I wasn't scared of this woman. If it was up to me, we would tear the whole house up.

She had the nerve to step closer to me and press her forehead to mine. "Like I said, where the fuck do you get off bringing your ass in here at this time of night? You didn't call nobody, and you certainly didn't have the permission. So, explain yourself, because you must think you are grown."

I took a step back and a deep breath. After exhaling, I turned my back on her and was on my way up the stairs. "Look, you're too angry right now to talk, and I'm tired, so let's say we do this some time in the morning? That way we will both have a clear head."

I bent over to pick my heels up, and this broad kicked me in the ass. I mean, dead in the center, too, right in the middle of my crack. I couldn't help but yelp out in pain.

She grabbed me by my hair, and I don't know where her strength came from, but she dragged me all the way across the room and into her bedroom. Once there, she opened a dresser drawer and pulled out a belt. "I'm gon' teach your little hot-ass a lesson, because you think it's a game."

I was struggling to get up, but she had my hair balled around her fist. All I could do was kick my legs and twist this way and that. I could barely see in front of me because the house was pitch dark. The only light came from her television.

I was thinking if she hit me with that belt, I was going to find something to hit her ass back with.

The first lash came across my back, and I screamed out because that shit hurt so bad. She didn't have one of those thick belts; she had a thin leather one that whipped through the air before tasting my skin and leaving a welt. The next lash came across my side, and the next across my back again. She was swinging the belt so fast and hard her breasts were knocking into each other and sweat was pouring from her forehead.

"I told you, little girl, that I was gon' show your ass a lesson. This is all you need. You're just fast, and that nature is calling you, but not in my muthafucking house. Ain't no bitch gon' be in here doing the most unless it's me, and that's that."

I was doing everything I possibly could to get away, but

126

she was not allowing that to happen. I felt blow after blow until I wrapped myself into a ball protectively and waited for the onslaught to stop.

She must have beat me for what seemed like five whole minutes. By the time she was finished, I had welts all over me and my body felt as if it had been stung by a thousand bumblebees.

"Now, get yo' ass up and get upstairs and clean up. I'm sick of your shit. If you fuck up one more time, I'm gon' beat you so good Harriet Tubman gon' roll over in her grave. I'm tired of playing with you, and I mean that."

I slowly climbed to my feet on wobbly knees. I felt sick and like I had just been taken advantage of. The tears sailed down my cheeks, and I couldn't stop the coughs from leaving my throat.

It took me forever to get to the top of the stairs. Once I did, I stood there for a minute and looked back down them. I had visions of running full speed and diving down them, hoping I would land the wrong way and my neck would snap. I yearned for the utter darkness and prayed God would take me away from the pains of the earth. I wanted to taste death. I needed the reaper. I was tired of living in that moment, and I didn't see the purpose to keep on moving forward.

When I felt arms wrap around my shoulders, I jumped from the sudden contact. I looked over and saw Jackie, and I could not believe she was there trying to comfort me. My lips began to quiver, and I felt cold. I let her put the blanket over my shoulders and I melted into her embrace. She kept on tucking my hair out of my face and kissing me on the forehead.

"It's going to be okay, Alexis. I got you, just please stop crying. Please, my sister," she whimpered, and I felt her tears wetting my forehead.

She took me into the upstairs bathroom and closed the door behind us. She sat me on the closed lid of the toilet and knelt down in front of me. I was too ashamed to look directly at her because I felt I was at my lowest point. I had been run into the ground and beaten by a woman whom we all despised. She had taken me down a couple notches into the abyss of darkness and self-loathing pain. Her brutality had squashed me as if I were an insect.

"Alexis, we need to get these clothes off of you because your blood is making them stick to you. Now, I'm going to run you some warm bath water, and you'll need to soak for a bit. I'm going to add some peroxide to it so it cleanses your wounds, and we'll go from there. Is that okay, baby?"

I nodded and stood up while she peeled my clothes away from me. It was just like she had said, they were sticking to the dried blood, and each time we pulled the articles down further I would wince in pain. The tears could not stop flowing. I felt so broken, and so vulnerable. I had never been loved my entire life. All I had ever known was pain and misery, ever since I came out of the womb. I just didn't understand the purpose in existing.

Finally, I was lowered into the tub, and to say it stung like hell would be an understatement. It actually sizzled and burned. It felt like something I had never felt before. Jackie was so calming, and I did not understand why she was being so nice to me, but I was extremely thankful for her in that moment. She took special care to wash my wounds, and she kept on wiping my tears away and kissing me on the forehead. Though I was in undeniable pain, she made me feel special, and I was in her debt for that.

Instead of going to my room that early morning, she took me into hers, wrapped in a robe, and laid me down on her bed. She rubbed my forehead until I drifted off, lying on my side because lying on my back was too painful.

I dreamed of my mom. I saw her face so clearly. She was smiling at me and trying to kiss my cheeks while I ran away from her with pigtails in my hair. Finally, she scooped me up and planted kisses all over my face, then rocked me in her arms. I felt so loved and special. *"You're my baby girl, and I will never leave your side again. You mean the world to me, and for you I will do anything, at any time."*

I woke up crying and smiling at the same time. I sat up in bed and noted the room was empty. I started to panic, thinking I had missed school, but then remembered it was the weekend. The last thing I wanted to do was piss off the Taylors again. I was worried the next time she would actually kill me.

Leah knocked on the door about ten minutes after I woke up and then poked her head inside. "Hey, girl. Can I come in?" she asked cautiously.

I tried my best to sit up and look normal. "Hey. Yeah, sure. Come on in."

She stepped into the room and closed the door behind her. She walked over to me, dropped to her knees, and started crying with her hands over her face.

I watched her rock back and forth for a little while before I scooted down to the floor and put my arms around her. "What's the matter, babe?"

She took her hands away from her face, and I noted her mascara ran down her cheeks in what looked like muddy rivers. "I'm going to kill that bitch, sis. I hate her. Look at what she did to you! I'm going to chop that whore up and feed her to a pig on a farm. I'm so tired of them bullying us!" she yelled, and I had to put my hand over her mouth.

She slapped it away and stood up. "No, fuck that, and fuck silence! Now, I'm telling you I don't care about me, but I love you, and no one is going to hurt you without me killing them.

I don't care what you say, or what anybody says. That bitch is dead, and if her ugly-ass man tries anything, I'm going to kill him, too."

I looked into her eyes and saw they were deranged and far off into the distance. She was seeing, but not seeing at the same time. They lowered until she looked almost sinister. I knew right then she was serious, and she would do anything for me. I could not lose that type of love. I just couldn't.

I stood up. "Wait a minute, Leah. Hear me out, okay? Please, will you do that?"

She gave me a look that said whatever I was about to say had better be good. I swallowed and became a little afraid of her. I started thinking about the majority of serial killers being white, then added in the fact she had been locked into a closet for the majority of her childhood. Then, when I looked into her eyes, I saw death, so I knew this was serious.

I walked up to her and grabbed her hands. "Baby, listen to me. I love you too much to let you throw your life away for me. I need you around just so I can know love exists. Now, we are way too smart to let this bitch get the better of us like this. What we need is a plan that will work in our favor and get us the hell out of here. Not separately, but together. I need you, do you hear me?" I kissed her on the lips, and her whole demeanor changed. She blushed and lowered her head. "Now, we need to come up with something that is foolproof, and that will bury this bitch so far into the ground even the worms will be two levels up from her."

The bedroom door opened up and Jackie came in. "Hey, guys. I don't mean to be eavesdropping, but I was, and I want in. I want to get out of here, too, and I think I got the perfect plan that will free all of us. However, we will need an adult to agree to take us in while they are investigating these people."

The first person who came to my mind was my cousin

Roman. I figured I could convince him to be that adult, and if not him, then Rosie's mom, or Rosie herself. We could always get an apartment, or we could lean on Prince or Li'l Chris. They were rolling in the dough, anyway. I figured they would be in a hurry to help.

"Or we could just run the fuck away together and say fuck this shit. Why are we staying here, anyway? Society doesn't give a fuck if we're running the streets or dead."

I was in deep thought, rubbing my chin. "Hey, I don't think we have to go to that extreme just yet. I have a few people that wouldn't mind taking us in, so don't worry about that."

"Wait, are you sure you mean us, or just you?" Leah asked, lowering her head.

"I mean all three of us, but that still depends on what plan Jackie has mulling around in her head."

Jackie put a finger to her mouth and told us to be quiet. She tiptoed to the door, closed and locked it. "All right, I know things, and I've seen things that are going to help us blow this pigeon coop. Listen to this, and this is what's going to spring us.

Chapter 13

Alexis

To be sure our plan would succeed, we waited three weeks to execute it, and it was the worst three weeks of my life. I was so anxious. They had me on a leash so tight I could barely breathe. My friendship with Rosie was getting weaker because we were barely able to see each other. Prince still made it his business to come by when he thought they weren't around, or he'd surprise me at school with gifts, but as far as us being able to be alone together for an extended period of time, that was out of the question. I don't know what it was, but he still held on. I remembered one of the conversations we'd had that blew my mind. We were parked in the parking lot of the school and had just come back from buying submarines. I could tell something was bothering him, and that affected my mood because I was genuinely starting to care about him.

I touched his hand. "Baby, what's the matter?"

He turned down the Brittany White CD and leaned his seat back a little. We were sitting in his brand-new Bentley Continental. He had just gotten it for his 18th birthday. "My Pop's at war real heavy right now with these Jamaican studs. We done lost a few members in our army, and I don't know. It just bothers me because my old man just got out the Feds, and now it's like plenty people are trying to kill him already. Everybody want to see King dead and riddled with bullets. Then, the other day, me and Li'l Chris were rolling out by the Stateway Projects and some niggaz put fifty shots in his car. They were trying to tear our heads off. Shit getting real hectic. Then I be missin' you and shit, but these people got you all hemmed up, so when I be needing you in my arms, I can't even have you because you're restricted from me. This is bananas, ma. I think I love you, or something like that." After saying this, he looked out of his window.

I swallowed because I didn't know what to say or how to act. I did not think he was capable of loving me, so I found that a little doubtful, although he did have me feeling some type of way.

I must have been silent for too long because he started to look uncomfortable. "Baby, I love you, too. And I'm sorry, but it's very little I can do about these people"

He nodded sadly. "Yeah, I know, but I'm going through a lot right now, and I need you so damn bad. And I ain't even talking about the fucking aspect, because you know I'm out here slaying hos, and that don't mean nothing to me. I need to hold you and be under you because you are the only one that make me feel good about life. You give me hope, and I don't know why."

He was making me feel all choked up and weak. I still didn't know what to say, though. No one had ever expressed their love to me before, so this was all new territory, and it was making me feel different. An indescribable different.

"I don't know, but it's about time for you to go back to class, so I guess I'll be back to pick you up later on after school lets out." He sounded so defeated.

I looked at the clock and noted I had about five minutes before I had to start heading inside. "Babe, what about these Jamaicans, though? Do you think it is wise for you to be rolling around in a flamboyant car while your father is at war with them?" I was concerned because he had me feeling some type of way, and I wanted him to be a constant in my life. At that time, we were losing so many people to gun violence in Chicago it was not hard to become a statistic, especially if your family was already at war with crazy rivals.

Everybody knew who King was, and Chris. Those dudes

were major heavy hitters in the Windy City and had half of it hooked on their heroin. They were enemy number one because they had forced a majority of the city to inject their drug at gunpoint. Whatever strategy they had, it worked, because almost everybody that was anybody worked under their regime, and they were filthy rich.

"Man, fuck them dread-heads. I'm not about to stop living because they want it with my father. What the fuck that shit got to do with me? That's what I be saying about these coward-ass niggaz: they are always going after the women and children and can't keep that shit stand-up enough to go at the man they are seeking. I'm not changing shit. If they want me, come and get me. I been balling since I was in Pampers, and I'm gon' keep balling. Niggaz want it with my old man, then it is what it is. I'm trying to wet every nigga with a dread in his head, Jamaican or not."

Damn, this boy had tears in my eyes because deep down I could see through that shit. I saw the worry in him. He didn't want to die, and he wasn't about that life. He was one of those sheltered thugs that got a crazy reputation because of who his father is, not by his own stripes. I didn't want him to act like he had to prove anything to me.

"Prince, why can't we just up and go away from here? Why can't we just disappear, baby, and get the hell out of Chicago?"

He shrugged his shoulders. "Where would we even go? I mean, the only time I've traveled was with my parents. All I know is Chicago." He looked over to me. "Why, where would you want to go?"

I didn't even know. I had never thought about that question ever being asked to me, but now that it had, I had a million places swarming in my mind. "Babe, we could go anywhere and just live life. I don't care where it is as long as we are together."

He smiled. "But what about the Taylors? What about your mom, baby, because you can't forget about her."

"And I never will. We'll go to another city and get ourselves together so when she comes home, she won't have any worries. I think most of our problems derive from this wicked-ass city."

The school bell sounded behind us, and I winced because I knew I was going to be in trouble. I was so tired of it all. I mean, I wanted to graduate, so I knew we'd at least have to wait until that happened, but after that I was down to go to the ends of the earth with him.

I started to think about Jackie and Leah, and I really wanted to bring them up to let him know they would be going along, but I didn't think it was the right time.

"I'll tell you what: we'll let you finish out this last year, and then we're out of here, baby. I'm thinking somewhere sunny like Miami or California. I just want everything to be new, but at the same time fast-paced. I want us to be able to shine bright and not have too many people get jealous because it's considered the norm for wherever we'll be. But I'm definitely down to do this with you. You just have to get rid of those Taylor people."

***

That was all I needed to hear to motivate me. I had to get out of their home, and I had to do it even before I left school. My cousin said he would take custody of me until I reached eighteen, or for as long as I wanted to be under his care. The Taylors were acting as if they didn't want to let me go and release me to him straight out. He'd told them they could keep the paychecks, but they still wanted to make things difficult.

136

We were huddled up in Jackie's room with the door locked. It had to be after two in the morning, and we were all up, wide-awake and eager. I was so giddy I could not sit still and Indian-style like they were. I kept on switching positions as I waited for Jackie to spell out the plan. We had the lights off and were using the light from my phone to see each other.

"All right, now, I'm telling you it's every other night like clockwork. You know Mr. Taylor works every other day at that one plant on third shift, right?"

Leah and I nodded, impatient for her to go on.

"Well, every night that he works there, Marshall comes to her room and they screw. And when I say they screw, I mean they get it on in the nastiest of fashions. She's a complete slut for him, and she does some things I'm not even comfortable mentioning." She shook her head. "But anyway, I've been using your phone, Alexis, to record all the things she does to him, and even that other boy that's way younger. And I've created a website I'm going to alert the authorities to, but before I do, I want to get some more raw footage and have her catch me recording it. That way she'll try to attack me, and you two will stop her. Then, before it's all said and done, we'll run away together and the police will know why. By the time your cousin brings us to them, months will have passed, and we'll all be close to our birthdays, so they'll just let him keep us until then. It's as simple as that. And in the middle of everything, they're going to pop that bitch's ass. So, what do you think?"

I didn't know what to think. I was all for it.

***

It was almost like clockwork. No more than five minutes after Mr. Taylor made his way out of the door, Marshall crept into the hallway and headed down the stairs. All three of us girls were huddled into the linen closet to the side of the bathroom, directly across from the stairwell. It was a cramped space, but we were on a mission. We were tired of being there, and it was time to enact the plan accordingly. Once we saw his fro disappear down the stairs, we waited about ten minutes before we followed behind him.

I swear it seemed like the stairs had never been squeakier. Every step we took sounded like they were screaming for Mrs. Taylor to kick Marshall out of her room. I didn't even think we'd get the chance to catch them in the act because the stairs were working as an alarm. Ugh, I was so glad when we got to the bottom. I had broken out into a sweat because I was so nervous. I hoped she didn't have that belt anywhere by her. I did not feel like getting beat all over again. That was for the birds.

As soon as we got to the bottom landing, we knew we were in the clear. I don't know if she was already riled up or what, but she was hollering out in bliss and the bed was going haywire. I crouched down by the door and stuck my ear against it. I could hear her moaning out his name and telling him to fuck her as hard as he could with his big, fresh dick, whatever that meant. Then I heard him growling like a damn bear.

Jackie crouched down by me and held a finger to her lips like we needed to be told to be quiet. I'm pretty sure it was quite obvious we knew we were on a mission. I'm just saying, I didn't understand why she needed to do that. She reached up and slowly turned the knob, opening the door, then she crawled into the room on all fours with us following close behind. I was so nervous my stomach was doing somersaults.

The bed sounded like kids were on top of it, jumping up and down.

Mrs. Taylor couldn't contain herself. "Oh my god, I love it when you fuck me like this. Please, baby, do mommy harder. Fuck me good, baby. I need it. Manhandle those titties you love so damn much!"

Their skins slapped into each other, sounding like they were giving a round of applause. Marshall grunted while the headboard knocked into the wall constantly. It smelled like heavy sweat and sex in the room. They had it so stuffy in there I could barely breathe.

Jackie slowly stood up in the corner of the room and held the phone over the bed. I must have watched her record them for a whole ten minutes before we heard Mrs. Taylor's voice.

"What the fuck is going on? What are you doing in here?"

Jackie was silent for a while. "Oh, I'm just recording you taking advantage of your foster kids and uploading it to your website. It shouldn't be long before the authorities see this and your ass is out. You're going down." She started laughing hysterically.

"Jackie, get out of here! What are you doing? Are you crazy or something?" Marshall said.

The next thing I knew, he fell onto the floor and Mrs. Taylor was scrambling to get out of the bed, keeping the sheets wrapped around her.

That's when Leah flipped on the lights and held up a phone of her own. "I gotcha, bitch!" she yelled, laughing and snapping picture after picture.

There was so much excitement going on that I didn't know where to look. Marshall was struggling to put his boxers on. Before he could slide them up his thighs, I saw he had a huge piece. It looked like somebody had been pulling on it all his life, because it hung past his balls. I was shocked and a little bit turned on. I wish I had known he was packing like that. I definitely would have figured out what to do with it. Even then

I had to touch myself for a moment.

I snapped out of my zone when Mrs. Taylor dived and tackled Jackie to the floor just as the younger kids came down the stairs.

"Get off of me you big, black, Precious-looking bitch! I can't breathe." I could barely make out her face because the sheet was all over it, along with Mrs. Taylor.

"Give me that phone before I kill you, little girl! And I'm not playing with you, either."

They struggled and Jackie tossed the phone across the bed. Leah dived for it and rolled to the floor beside me.

"Girl, snap out of it. Come on, let's go! Now!" she hollered.

I shook the cobwebs from my brain and snapped into action. I tried to pull Mrs. Taylor off of Jackie, but she was choking her to death by this time.

"Get off of me, bitch! I can't breathe," she said with her voice cracking up. She kicked her legs in a moot attempt to free herself.

I tried again to pull the fat woman off of her. This time she turned around and pushed me so hard I flew into the dresser. This made Leah go nuts. She screamed out something, then charged at the woman full-speed, swinging her arms, punching her three times in the face and busting her nose. That was all the diversion Jackie needed to free herself. She wiggled from under the woman and stood up. Leah tossed her the phone and she ran out of the room, knocking over one of the younger boys on her way out.

Mrs. Taylor caught one of Leah's punches and pulled her to her and head butted her straight in the chest, knocking the wind out of the girl. Leah fell onto her back with her eyes wide open.

I reached down and slapped Mrs. Taylor so hard she spit

140

out across the mirror. I backed up and threw up my guards, then thought about it and decided against that. I pulled Leah by the hand, she was just starting to get her wind back. We staggered out of the room and the house. Rosie was waiting on us at the curb. We jumped into her Jeep and she floored it away from their place.

T.J. & Jelissa

Chapter 14

Alexis

"Yeah, we got they ass. They definitely ain't gon' be able to fight this custody suit with none of y'all. I think they gon' concede to keep receiving them checks and just let y'all stay here with me," Roman said as he looked at the footage Jackie had just uploaded to the website.

We were all sitting in his living room a bit shell-shocked, them more than me because they did not believe he was okay with them staying there. I knew they were good. The only thing I was worried about was this new high, yellow female walking around his house in damn near nothing. I did not like her, and I made sure she saw the looks I gave her to cement my point. The last I remembered, he was telling me he was single and without a spouse, so who in the hell was she? I needed to know.

I waited until breakfast the next morning. My cousin had gotten up pretty early to throw down on the stove. After he called us all down, plates were sat in front of us with triple cheese omelets, French toast, turkey sausages, and even a bagel. While I poured me a big glass of orange juice, I looked across the table at this new female and stared her down.

"Uh, my name is Alexis, as you know. And this is Jackie, and that is Leah. Now, who might you be?" I sat my glass down so hard it spilled some of the juice. I didn't like her being there. This was my people. I didn't feel like sharing him with nobody just yet. After all, we were still in the stage of getting to know each other.

She dropped her fork into the syrup surrounding her French toast and tried to pick it up without getting the liquid on her fingers. I could tell she was nervous, and I was happy about that. This bitch was sitting at the table in a wife beater so tight I could clearly see her nipples through it. Then she had the audacity to be walking around in booty shorts that hugged her little muffin. She was shooting for all of his attention, and I wasn't having that.

"I'm sorry, I thought I'd already introduced myself."

"Well, you didn't. So, who are you?"

She started to bite on her lower lips. Another thing I didn't like about her was the fact she seemed to be only a few years older than me, if not my age. I looked at this bitch as competition for the attention I needed, and I wasn't going for that.

"My name is Arianna, and your mother is like a mother to me."

I must have scooted back my chair so far I crashed into the refrigerator behind me. Did she just say she was a friend of my mother's? No, she said my mother was like a mother to her. Now I was really getting jealous, because not only was she looking to steal my cousin, but my mother, as well. "Come again?"

"Well, it's a long story, but I'll try to be brief."

"Nall, take your time. We ain't got nowhere to be, do we, ladies?"

They lowered their heads to their plates and tried to act as if they hadn't heard me. I knew I was acting out of character, but I was floating on a level of stress that had me running on fumes. I had not slept in three days, and I hadn't eaten in almost the same length of time. On top of that, I was worried about Prince and still trying to figure out what we were going to do about the Taylors. I missed my mom, and I loved my cousin and wanted to get to know him before he started any relationship with anybody. And on top of that, I was worried this high yellow-ass female was going to steal all of the attention and make him not want to even get to know me.

So yeah, I was acting out a little bit, but I felt I had every damn right to be. My life was a whirlwind, and it was messing me up.

"Well, before I was born, you mother and my mother were best friends. May I speak openly, because some of the details are pretty grim?"

I nodded. "Yeah, these my girls. Keep it one-hunnit. We're listening."

"Well, they also had the same pimp, this dude named Jaheim. He is also my father. Him and your mother were high school sweethearts, and they lived together in the Stateway Projects way before they met my mom. Your mom used to work the avenue, and after a short period of time, my dad picked up another worker, which turned out to be my mom. Anyway, they worked together for a spell until my dad got violent and beat your pregnant mother so bad she lost her baby at that time. At the same time, my mom was pregnant with me. She fell head over heels for my father, and he turned her onto first crack, and then heroin. Long story short, I was born addicted to both, and by that time caring for me became so overwhelming my mom gave up and killed herself." She paused as the tears fell from her eyes.

"But your mother stepped up to the plate, and she cared for me and paid my doctors' bills. She did everything she could do until she was taken away in handcuffs for a crime she did not commit. She has always been the only mother I have known, and I think the world of her. I really do." She paused to sip from her orange juice. "She asked your cousin, Roman, if he would take me in, and he agreed. He knew my mother, as well. I went through so many traumatic experiences at my old foster home that I couldn't take it anymore."

"So you see, Alexis, she's just like us," Jackie said,

reaching across the table and placing her hand on top of mine. I was trying my best to feel some kind of sympathy for her, but all I kept on thinking about was she was saying my mother was basically her mom, and she was traipsing around way too comfortable around my cousin's house, so I could only imagine she was feeling as if he were her family as well. I still didn't want to share my people. This girl was too damn beautiful, and I knew it would be easy for my mother or my cousin to forget all about me with her around. I just didn't like it.

Roman came into the kitchen and knelt down beside her. "Are you okay, li'l momma?" Then he stood up, pulled her to her feet, and wrapped his arms around her after kissing her on the forehead.

That made my stomach turn quite a bit from jealousy. I kept my mouth closed because I didn't know what to say or if I should have said anything to begin with. I started to miss Prince, and wondered when the next time that him and I would get together. Suddenly, I needed the presence of a male that only cared about me.

I continued to watch Roman console Arianna, and then Jackie was getting in on the mix. My stomach turned for the second time, and I scooted away from the table. I didn't like her, and there was nothing anybody could do to change my mind. I needed to get out for a minute. I needed Prince. I needed to see him bad. Now that I didn't have the Taylors breathing down my neck, I felt I would be able to see him more.

I stepped out onto the patio and pulled my phone out, dialing Prince's number. It rang and rang and finally sent me to his voicemail. I felt defeated. I told him as soon as he got this message to call me because I needed him.

Standing in my cousin's backyard gave me a chance to

breathe in some fresh air. I found myself pacing back and forth as the sun shined bright and warm onto my forehead. I kept on shaking out my arms and rolling my neck around on my shoulders, trying to loosen up because I felt so damn tense all over. I didn't know what I was about to do, or how long I was planning on staying under his roof. As comfortable as I thought I would feel there, I was actually feeling the opposite. I mean, on the one hand it was cool to be away from the Taylors, and I wasn't even sure how long it would be before they came either looking for us or raising a fuss. I hoped they'd surrender their control and bow out gracefully. We had enough evidence against Mrs. Taylor to send her directly to jail, and the state would definitely take their license away. The only thing that bothered me with the situation was I didn't think she would be able to explain to her husband where we were and why we'd left. I mean, what could she have said short of snitching on herself? I knew she was way too smart for that. Oh no, she'd find a way to flip this all around, so the way she'd do it worried me some.

I also thought about Leah and Jackie being along for the ride with me, and I didn't know exactly how that was going to pan out. I started to miss Prince, and I wanted to be alone with him. If he had asked me to run away in the next hour, I would have, and I don't think I would have told anybody anything. I would have simply left.

I took another deep breath as two blue jays flew over my head and landed on the telephone wire that ran along the ally behind my cousin's house. I envied them because of how free they were to roam. If they got tired of being in one place for too long, all they had to do was fly away and find greener pastures.

I wrapped my arms around my body and pressed my back against his white picket fence. I had so much going on in my mind that I felt sick almost.

Roman stepped onto the patio and closed the door behind him. He walked to the backyard where I was and hugged me. "Hey now, baby, what's the matter?" he cooed, pressing me up against his chest.

I wrapped my arms around him and inhaled. He smelled so damn good. I hated the way I felt so protected in his arms. I felt like he really cared about me, and he didn't even really know me. He made me feel so small, and so secure, but even worse than those two was the jealousy.

I closed my eyes tightly and held onto him and imagined I was the only one there. It was just me and him, and I didn't have to share, and he would protect me and raise me to be his princess. He would always put me first, and he would never let any female come before me. I would never feel alone because he'd never allow that to happen. He'd live every day just to love me, and it would be all we'd need.

"Roman, I don't like that girl in there, and I don't want to share you or my mother with her. I need you all to myself until my mom gets home. I don't want you to love her, too." I forced my face further into his chest and tightened my grip on his waist.

He leaned down and kissed me on the forehead. "Aw, baby girl, is that what you're out here tripping about?"

I nodded.

"You don't have to worry about that, Alexis. I am just doing your mother a favor when it comes to her. She asked me to look over her until she got on her feet. Besides, me and her mother used to have this little brief thing, so I felt kind of obligated to step in and up to the plate. But make no mistake, nobody comes before you. You're my baby girl, and you have to know that. I been trying to get into your life since you've been alive, and those people have made it so damn difficult.

But now that I got you, I'm gon' hold you down like I'm supposed to. You understanding me right now, huh?" He took my arms from around him and pushed me back a little bit so he could look into my face.

I was too damn shy to look directly into his eyes. I didn't know what was wrong with me, so I faced him, but I kept on looking at the ground until he tilted my chin upward. Only then did our eyes meet, and I melted into a puddle. I saw so much sincerity within them. He really loved me, and that made me feel special. I didn't feel as alone. Sometimes in life I could be in a room with a thousand or more people and still feel all alone. I was tired of feeling hurt and down. I just needed somebody to care, and somebody to put me first in their life. I wanted to know I mattered, and I guess I needed to matter to a man because it was in that field I felt so estranged.

I stepped back into his embrace and wrapped my arms around his waist. "Roman, I don't want to share you. I know I said that before, but you have no idea how much I truly mean that. I feel like you're the only man in my life that actually cares about me, and I don't want to lose you before we get to know each other. I will do anything for your love, and I'll do anything to outdo that girl in there. I don't know her, and I don't feel I should have to share my people with her. My mother is not her mother, she's mine. And she's not your baby girl, I am."

I knew I was sounding like a brat, but I didn't care. Just feeling his arms wrapped around me had my inner child coming to the forefront. I felt like a little girl. I needed to feel that way because I had never been given the chance before.

He held me tighter, and I could feel his chin stubble on the side of my forehead. "Baby girl, then just tell me what you want me to do, and if it will make you feel all better, I will. I feel like I don't owe anybody in that house anything. You are my number one priority, so if you want me to go in there and kick everybody out, all you have to do is say the word, and it's a done deal. I mean that."

I thought long and hard about being on some straight selfish shit, too. I mean, I imagined me finally being able to live in a home where I could feel safe and there was a male there that loved me unconditionally, and I almost caved in and told him to go in there and kick everybody out and to the curb. But then I got to thinking about my girls and the struggle we'd just gone through together. I started thinking about pissing my mom off, and that made me feel some type of way. I wanted her to love me and not be disappointed with me. I was already curious as to how she was going to take the news about me running away from the Taylors. Hopefully she'd understand that, though, because we had the videos and more than one great excuse, plus I'd ran home to family. She'd have to see the logic in that, and I was hoping she'd just be happy I was safe and sound.

I took a step back. "No, it's cool, Roman. You don't have to kick them all out. I mean, that would be evil, right?" I lowered my head and thought how that would look, then I shook it. That would have been a cold-blooded move, and God would have for sure gotten me if I was at the center of his decision to throw them to the streets.

I looked up to him and directly in his eyes. "Can you just make sure you always love me, and you don't neglect me because of that yellow girl? Do you promise we'll have a strong relationship, no matter what?" I asked, really hoping we would. I needed him. I needed that male within my life for guidance and love. I felt lost this whole time without having that kind of presence. My father never made the effort, and my grandfather was horrible altogether, so I was deprived of that kind of affection. Now that I had it standing in front of me, I

150

didn't want to let it go.

He nodded. "I promise, babe. It's you and I, and I got your back. Don't you worry about a damn thang, you hear me?" He rubbed my chin, then gave me a kiss on the cheek. Once again, I melted.

***

We walked back into the house with his arms around my shoulders. I felt so damn good, I wanted to stay that way forever if I could. The only thing that broke me away from him was the ringing of my phone. I looked at the face and saw Prince's picture pop up. I can't even lie, I felt giddy. I turned and kissed Roman on the cheek, and then ran back outside, answering it. "Hello, baby, is that you?" I said, feeling the waterworks come.

"Yeah. What up, boo? I just got your message. What's the biz?" I could hear music in the background, which told me he was rolling around the city in his car. I started imagining myself in the passenger seat and yearned for him.

"Prince, it's been a bunch of bullshit that went on with the Taylors, and we had to run away from there. I'm staying with my cousin right now, and he super chill. I need to see you, baby. I mean, I need to see you right now. Is that possible?" I said this last part low with my hopes so high they were somewhere in outer space.

He was silent for a minute. "Yo, I can come scoop you right now, but if I do, you gon' have to roll out of town with me so I can conduct this business. I ain't gon' say much over this phone, but I'm telling you, boo, that it's serious. Or you can wait and I'll be back in a couple days."

I heard what sounded like a female's voice in the background, and my defenses went all the way up. "Hell nall, you can come get me right now. Whatever business you have to conduct, I'm going to be right by your side because that's my place. So, how long is it going to take you to get here?" I asked impatiently. I was wondering who that female was I was hearing in the background. I knew he had better not bring her with him or I was about to tear some shit up. Win, lose, or draw, I was willing to fight for my man, and that was that.

"I'll be there in about a half an hour. Make sure you're ready, because I'm going to blow the horn a few times and expect you to run right out. Oh, and you have to give me the address. Where y'all at?"

Chapter 15

Alexis

This boy had so many cars I was losing count. When he pulled up in a platinum BMW M-5 sitting on 26-inch Davins, I couldn't do nothing but shake my head. I must have broken my neck trying to get off that porch. I wanted to hug my man and kiss on his lips. I had missed him so damn bad.

So, imagine my face when I got down to the car and this super-thick Asian and Black woman stepped out in a Givenchy dress that hugged her curves so tight even I was mildly turned on. Her hair fell way past her back, and her booty looked like she was competing with Kim K.

She had the nerve to be sitting in the passenger's seat. She got out to dust some crumbs from her lap. It was evident they had eaten because there were Chipotle bags in the front, and one in the back I assumed was for me. I stuck my hand on my hip and rolled my eyes. I was waiting for her to get into the backseat, but she sat her pretty ass back in the front and closed her door. I thought about running into the house and getting a knife to slice this broad up. She looked like she could fight, too, and I wasn't secure in my stand-up game at that time, but I knew how to poke a bitch.

I refused to get into the backseat. I walked around to Prince's window and knocked on the glass. He lowered it and blew the weed smoke past my face.

"What's up, baby? Why you ain't got in yet?"

He had on a pair of Ray Bans that made him look so damn fine I almost dropped my guard and said fuck that front seat because I didn't want to be left behind. I could only imagine what him and her could do without me. She was so fine that every time I looked at her, I felt like I was getting an erection, and I didn't even have that tool. Her dress was cut low enough to show the majority of her tits off. The only thing I yearned to see was the nipple, because the rest of the breast was on full display. She looked at me and licked her sexy lips. I felt intimidated.

I ignored her. "Prince, why am I sitting in the backseat? I thought I was your woman?" I whispered.

The female smiled and then laughed to herself. She picked up her drink and drank from the straw. She looked so secure in her position. I could tell she wasn't worried about nothing, and that made me feel insecure, especially when she touched his digital interface and turned to what she wanted to hear on the radio. He barely even let me do that, and even then, there was always a small argument that ensued.

He snickered. "Babe, you tripping. I can tell by the way you looking at her you're ready to attack, huh?" He looked back to the woman, and then back to me.

She started rummaging through her expensive handbag. "Boy, you better tell her before I bring this old project living up out of me." She didn't even bother to look up at us. She was too busy trying to locate something in her bag.

He started laughing briefly. "Baby, get in the car and chill out. I'll explain what's good when you get back there."

I reluctantly listened to him, although I felt like snapping the fuck out. I didn't understand why she couldn't get in the backseat. He had me feeling like a second-class citizen. How in the hell was I supposed to be his woman, but he had another, shapelier woman sitting in my place? I wondered if he was trying to tell me something, and that irritated me all the more.

I got into the backseat and moved the bag of food to the side. As soon as my door closed, he peeled away from the curb, knocking me backward. I hurried up and put on my seatbelt. Knowing him, he was going to try and show out in front of this new dame, and I wasn't about to risk my life in the process.

We were all quiet until he turned onto the expressway and took the car to top speeds. He turned the music all the way up, so loud it felt like somebody was kneeing me in the head. My nosy-ass wanted to find out who this girl was, but I knew that was a damn difficult task, being that the music was so loud.. He didn't turn it back down until we got to the airport, and the shapely woman turned around in her seat with her hand out.

"How are you doing, sweetheart? And for the record, this is my son. My name is China, and he has told me so much about you."

His mother. *His mother*. Damn, I could not believe his mother was that gorgeous or held herself so poised. I felt like a damn fool now. I blushed and shook her hand.

"I'm so sorry. My name is Alexis, and it is a pleasure to meet you."

He popped the trunk, and the man came out and helped her with her Gucci luggage. I waited until she was all the way inside before I reached over and punched him in the arm so hard my wrist went numb for a second or two.

He swerved the car a little bit and almost hit an old man. The old man slammed his cane down on the hood of the car and shook his fists at us. Prince rolled down the window. "Say, you old geezer, you better quit hitting my whip with that wooden cane or else it's gon' be trouble."

The old black man waved him off and slowly made his way across the street. It took him a little while, but he finally got there. Only then did he turn around, drop his pants, and pull his diaper down to moon us. I could not help laughing and beating my fist against the dashboard.

Prince didn't think it was funny. He zoomed away from the curb and mugged me as if he were ticked off.

"Damn, baby, what's the matter with you?" I asked, feeling a little down now.

He pulled up past the lights and parked his car and got out. I watched him look down at his hood and run his hand across the top of it. Then he frowned up his face and got back into the whip. "Fuck!"

"Everything okay?"

"Hell nall. That old dude put a dent in my shit, so I'm about to go get me a new one and trade this one in. I can't be rolling around all busted and shit. That ain't my style," he said, storming away from the curb.

I stood up in my seat, trying to see what the damage was, but I couldn't see anything. "Why didn't you tell me that was your mother when I first came out?" I asked.

He smiled. "Because I wanted you to squirm a little bit. Besides, how could you not tell?"

I shrugged my shoulders. "I don't know. I just thought she was some video vixen you'd picked up along the way. You know how you do. That lady is way too pretty to have a son your age. I thought she was working that throw back on you," I snickered.

He grunted. "Man, shorty, you sounding real weird right now. I just told you that's my moms. Now you got all these crazy-ass images going through my head. You ain't right."

I was laughing so hard by this time that my stomach hurt. I rubbed his arm. "Oh, I'm sorry, baby. I didn't mean it like that. But your mother is beautiful. That's a blessing, for real."

"Thank you. Now, like I was telling you on the phone, I got some business I gotta take care of up north, and it gotta be done by tomorrow. You sure you gon' roll out with me? It might be a little dangerous."

I raised an eyebrow. "How dangerous are we talking?"

He stepped his foot onto the gas a little harder. "That

depends on how much I can trust you."

I gave him a look that told him I was all in and I had his back. "Does that answer it for you?"

He nodded. "All right. Well, don't freak out, but I think I have to body a nigga because they are fucking up one of my Pop's work sites. This nigga been coming up short for a little while now, and I'm supposed to be in charge of his operation. He trying to play me like a softy, and I ain't with that shit, so I gotta put in a little work."

I swallowed. "And you're sure you have to kill him, though?" I didn't know how I felt about that. I got to thinking about my mother and her being in prison. I didn't want to wind up in the same position. After all, I felt I hadn't even had the chance to properly enjoy life. I got to imagining her coming home and me going inside. It would be like we were switching places or something.

The killing aspect of things didn't bother me as much. I was so used to seeing or hearing about someone being murdered in Chicago that death became second nature to me. We all had to go sometime, and every person wouldn't be blessed to go out in their sleep. Some of us are destined to be shot or stabbed to death. I mean, personally, I hoped when I went out, I was sleeping and pain wasn't a part of the equation. I didn't know whether there was a Heaven or Hell, but I felt we had to go somewhere next. This life had to be a gateway into another one. As painful as living on Earth was, I just didn't see it as being final.

"What if I did have to? Would you ride with me?"

Before I could stop to think things over thoroughly, I said, "Prince, I'm down for whatever you're down for, and I got your back just as long as you don't get me killed."

T.J. & Jelissa

Chapter 16

Tiny

If someone would have told me back in the day that a white man would have bent me over his desk while he spanked my ass and called me every racist name in the dictionary, I would have probably lashed out and smacked that person, but that's exactly the position I was in.

I had just watched him lock his office door, and he slowly unloosened his tie. The order was for me to be bent over his desk with the small pink gown on that he'd bought me. It was so short that every time I breathed in or out, it rose and showed off the cheeks of my ass. I was told to have myself wet and ready for him. So, as I watched him take his tie off, I played between my legs and spread the lips of my goodie box.

I couldn't believe how revved up I was, but there was something about how taboo everything was that had me going. I didn't like playing this slave shit. And by I, I meant my upper half, but I couldn't tell my clitoris that. My jewel was throbbing and dropping from excitement.

I wondered if any of those sistahs back in the day used to get turned on by their slave masters. I refused to believe that all of them weren't with that kinky stuff. If I had been alive back then, I think I would have just rolled with the punches. I mean, what was the difference of fucking in a cotton field or in a cool house. I ain't saying I would have been a house nigga or whatever, but I wouldn't have been all the way against the freaky shit that was going on back then. I'm just saying. And I know a lot of sistahs wouldn't have been, either.

He walked behind me as my fingers slid into my box. I was so wet my essence dripped down and off of my wrist onto his carpet. I spread my legs wider to give him a better view.

"Mm, that's what I'm talking about right there, Brown Sugar. Let me see all of those goodies. That's why I bought you, because you are prime, baby." He groaned, and I could feel his hand on my butt, stroking. "Tell me, Brown Sugar. Tell me, what do you want your master doing to you right now?"

I put my fingers as far into me as they would go until I was sitting on the palm of my hand. "I want you to spank me, daddy, because I been a bad girl and did what you told me not to do." I moaned and slid my fingers out and then in again.

He squeezed my booty and tapped it, just a taste. "And what was that, baby? What did I tell you not to do that you have wound up doing anyway?"

I heard the familiar sounds of him unbuckling his belt, and that got me excited. I don't know what it was about the scenario that was getting me off, but it was definitely working. "I can't keep my hands from between my legs. I have to touch the naughty place you told me not to touch. I yearn for the feel of my fingers inside of my cave, daddy, and I don't know what to do." I rolled my middle finger around my jewel, then pinched it. My nipples were so hard they felt like they were about to pop off my chest.

I yelped out loud when I felt him grab a handful of my hair and yank my head backward. "What is it that got you so riled up? Have you been carrying on with one of those other coons in the fields? Huh? You been rolling around with one of those niggers behind my back?"

That was the only part I didn't really like. I didn't like when he started the nigger talk and calling my people coons and shit. That's when I started to feel guilty and like I was betraying all humanity. It was like the worse he spoke about my people, the hotter it got him. I only had a few more weeks to clean his office before my community custody hearing came up, to which he sat on the board. All he had to do was give them the nod and I would be long gone away from here. I was so damn close.

I nodded my head. "Un-huh. I can't help myself, daddy. I see their black skin with the sweat dripping off of it and I gets to getting all kinds of excited. I can't control my desires, and before you know it, I got my fingers up in my juice box. And it feel so good, daddy," I said in my best slave voice.

He gripped my hair harder and brought his face to my ear. "But I told you they were off limits. I told you that you were my property, and everything you are, everything you is, belongs to me. Now, since you have taken it upon yourself to displease me, you have to be punished. Do you understand that?"

I nodded and he licked my face from my chin all the way up to my hairline. I didn't know if I was feeling that. His breath smelled like coffee, and I never got into drinking that stuff. He took my head and pressed it to his desk, then raised his hand and brought it down onto my ass cheek, catching me off guard. I yelped in pain.

"Keep spreading those lips, gurl. I want to see inside of you while you are punished."

I spread myself open further with my two fingers. He slammed his hand down onto my right butt cheek, then squeezed it, then did the same with the left. Before it was all said and done, he was giving me steady lashes, one after the next. It went on for about five minutes.

After he finished his assault, I was so wet it pooled down my thighs onto my ankles. My legs were shaking because I was horny, I needed to be screwed in the worst way. I needed him to put it to me, because my blood was boiling. My jewel was on fire.

He knelt down in back of me, spread my ass cheeks, and

ran his tongue up and down in between them. I started to go crazy. Then he trapped my jewel with his lips and sucked with all of his might, and that made me holler out so loud I knew his secretary had to hear us on the other side of the door. I smelled my essence all in the air, and that turned me on all over again.

He slid his fingers into me and started to stab them in and out at full speed while he sucked on my pearl. By this time, I was crying and begging for him to fuck me.

I was calling myself a nigger. Ain't that a bitch?

"Please, daddy, fuck me right now. I need you so bad. Your little nigger girl needs you inside of her. Punish me because I was wrong," I whimpered.

I felt him stand up. "You want this white dick in your black mouth, little girl? Huh? Do you?" he asked with a handful of my hair. He started to rub his piece all over my face, missing my mouth on purpose. I felt his juices smearing my eyelids and for some reason that made me yearn to taste him.

"Yes, daddy, give it to me. Give me your –"

Before I could even finish, he'd slid it past my lips, and I found myself sucking him for dear life. I mean, if anyone would have seen me, they would have been embarrassed because my head moved up and down a mile a minute as I took him to the back of my throat again and again.

He stood on the tip of his toes and fucked my mouth like he loved it, and I made it as wet and tight as possible for him. I used my tongue and pulled with my lips. I wanted to taste his juices bad.

Finally, he pulled it out of my mouth, causing a loud popping sound. It caught me off guard, and my head was still moving. He flipped me onto my back and spread my legs, then guided his dick deep into me, and I felt him soak into my center. I put my own knees onto my shoulders and let him pound my goodies for all I was worth. And he did, too. I even wrapped my hands around his waist to make him dive deeper. I was so wet I could literally hear his pole sliding in and out of me.

The shower that followed directly after was amazing. I always liked the fact he had a personal bathroom and shower connected directly to his office. I let the beads of water pour over my skin while he ate my goodies down low. I put one foot onto the rim of the tub while he wrapped his arm around my right thigh and smeared his face all up into my center of pleasure. I couldn't close my mouth, and some of the noises I made were right out of the jungle.

***

Back in my room, Deena gave me a massage that felt so good it was like I was in Heaven. She did it firmly and thorough. She knew what I had going on with the warden, and she had never judged me. Every time I'd leave his office, she'd kissed my body from head to toe and gave me the gift of one of her massages that drove me crazy. I don't know exactly what I felt for her, but I did know she was in my heart, and I cared about her dearly.

***

Sometimes, when you pray hard and believe in the One that stands in judgment of us all, the best things happen for your own benefit. I had been having a horrible week where it felt like very day something was going wrong. I kept on getting into minor arguments with the girls around the compound over the stupidest of things. I guess I was just ready to go, ready to be done with the prison scene, because everything and everybody got on my nerves. I hated the whole ordeal collectively.

I wanted back out into that free world. I wanted to be around my daughter again. I missed her so much. I had not heard from her since the last time she visited, and I wondered if maybe I had done something to keep her away from me. I secretly yearned for her love and thought about her every single day. I wanted to get home so I could start motherhood. I owed her so much for being away from her for her entire life thus far.

I missed Arianna as well, and I knew I would do whatever it'd take to be there for her, also. To me she was just as much my daughter as Alexis. I remembered way back when she was hooked up to feeding tubes and barely able to survive on her own. Just a small infant in a world of pain and neglect. I remembered how her mother had given up on her and chosen to take her own life. I remembered how that had made me feel. I thought she was a coward, a low life after that. I lost all respect for her as a woman. How could any mother give up on her child? How could any mother choose to stop living when their child was on their deathbed and in need of love and support? I didn't get it, nor did I get her, and I didn't want to after she told me she was giving up on her daughter. From the day those words came out of her mouth, I promised myself I would always be there for Arianna, and I would view her as my own child. That was a promise I intended to keep.

But, as I was saying, everything was going horrible that week, it seemed, and I felt I was at my wit's end. I was ready to snap out or lash out at somebody just to blow some steam. I remembered waking up that Friday morning in such a state of agitation I felt like screaming.

My aunt had always told me if I ever woke up feeling as

if I wanted to kill somebody, I was to get down on my knees and talk to Jesus so he could talk directly to God for me. Well, it was one of those days. I was feeling annoyed and a whole lot irritated. I felt that if I got into an argument with any female that day, I would surely try to kill her, and I'd just have to deal with the consequences later. I didn't even want to get out of the bed, but I had to go to work that morning, so I was forced to begin the process of getting ready.

I placed both feet onto the floor and then slid to my knees with my hands clasped together in prayer. I needed to talk to Jesus. I needed his strength. I wasn't in the mood to be called a bunch of niggers and to be made a sex slave while a racist man took advantage of my body. I didn't feel like I could have played that role that day. I felt weak and on edge. I just needed to talk to him so he'd know I was in need of his blood, of his security.

I closed my eyes and took a deep breath. "Lord Jesus, I pray You hear my prayers. I am feeling so weak today, and so above it all. I need Your help and Your guidance to get me through, because I cannot do this alone. I am tired of the strife and tribulations this prison and life brings. You know I am innocent, and I have more than served my time. I have done everything that has been asked of me, yet I am still here, yearning to be set free. Father God, I do not know how You were strong enough to sustain Your stripes and the things You have in order for us to be able to walk in Your blood, but I thank You for enduring it. And I thank You for loving us all. Father, I pray You open these gates and release me into the community where I belong. Help me to be able to protect my daughters and be able to be a strong role model in their lives. Bless me, Jesus. Help me, Jesus. I pray through the vessel of You. I ask these things and all things within Your Holy and Precious name. Amen."

I stood up and felt so much better, like a weight had been lifted off my shoulders. I started to get ready, singing a gospel tune to myself and probably shaking my butt more than I should have, but it was all good and in the name of Him.

***

I got worried when I got to the warden's office and his secretary was nowhere in sight. He directed me into his office by my arm and closed the door. I looked all around the room for kinky toys or paraphernalia, but I saw none. He seemed as if he was in a good mood, and that had me all kinds of suspicious. He made me sit down while he took his suit jacket off.

I looked out the window, and it was raining so hard I could barely see out of it. Lightning flashed across the sky, followed by thunder sounding with a big boom. I remembered wondering if my daughter was inside or out in the rain. I wondered if she was safe and sound. I wondered the same about Arianna. Then I thought about how it felt the last time I had been out into the free reign of the world. Not prison rain, but free world rain. Trust me, there is a difference. But I could not remember, and that made me sad.

The warden sat behind his desk and took a big jelly doughnut out of the box on his desktop. He reached across the table and handed it to me. I declined and pushed his hand away. I might have been a freak, but I was still not into eating out of somebody's hand. I reached across his desk and opened the box and pulled out a big glazed doughnut. It looked so good that before I bit into it, my stomach started growling and making noises.

"Oh, so it's that one you like, huh?" he asked, placing the jelly doughnut back into the box.

I wasn't paying him no mind. It had been so long since I had eaten a doughnut from the streets that all I heard was smacking from my mouth. That boy tasted awesome, too. I mean, it hit every taste bud I had inside of me. After I finished it, I ran my tongue around my teeth, relishing in the aftertaste.

The warden stood up and folded his arms behind his back. "Well, Zivial, I think it's time you finally get out of this place and onto greener pastures."

I was trying to swallow, but couldn't. I didn't know if I was hearing him right. Then my mind started to play tricks on me. I started thinking he was setting up a scenario for a slave master releasing his slave to the north, and I was figuring he wanted me to join in on the playing, but I didn't feel like it. "I beg your pardon?" I asked, disinterested.

He smiled and continued to pace the room. "You heard me. I am ready to let you go into the community. I think we have to cut all ties because you are becoming dangerous."

Now I knew this fool was playing or losing his mind. How the hell was I becoming dangerous? I was hoping he hadn't reread my file and was starting to get cold feet. I hated that they painted me as a monster. I had not killed anybody other than myself, it seemed. How could I have possibly been viewed as a danger to him? I wanted to know. I also wanted to know if this was his way of firing me. "What are you talking about, sir?"

He kept on pacing, and then abruptly stopped in front of me with tears in his eyes. "Zivial, I am falling too madly in love with you. It is getting to the point where I am yearning for your body. I get hard when I am with my wife and I think about that bronzed skin of yours. I want you all the time, and you have some of the best pussy I have ever had in my life. I fiend for it, the way it wraps around my dick and squeezes the life out of me, milking me and pouring out its gelatinous fluids. You are a hot piece, my Brown Sugar momma, and you are like heroin to me. I have to kick you cold turkey or wallow in your grasp for an eternity."

I was looking at this fool with my head turned slightly to the side, thinking he had lost his damn mind and the best part of his common sense. I didn't know what the hell he was talking about or where he was going with it, so I just stayed the course and held my silence.

He came and knelt down in front of me, placing his hands on each one of my knees. "Baby, I'm going to do you the biggest favor in the world. I'm going to release you to the community, and you'll have a job driving limousines. You'll stay in the Change House for 90 days, and after that you will be a free woman all together. I have a partner that runs the program over there, and he knows all about you. You keep him happy and he'll keep you on the streets and out of prison. It's a two-way street, one hand washes the other. Do you understand? If you play your cards right you may not have to do the full 90 days, but that will be between you and him. My job is to prepare the paperwork and get the bigwigs to sign off on your release. You do realize I am going above and beyond for you?"

I didn't know what to say, so instead I ripped off his pants and gave him the best head of his life.

***

That night I could not sleep at all. I could not believe I would be leaving prison after so long. I wanted to scream out my joy at the top of a mountain. I wanted to call my daughter and tell her that I was coming home. I wanted to call Roman and do the same. I was so anxious I didn't know what to do. I hated that it was a Friday because that meant I would have to go the whole weekend without knowing the answers from the higher ups. It was going to be impossible to sleep, but I felt the worst part was already over. At least I hoped so.

That night I talked to Jesus so much I was sure he was about ready to tell me to shut up.

***

Sunday afternoon I got a visit from Arianna and Roman. When I saw them, I almost broke my neck trying to run to them. I got to Roman first, and he picked me up in the air and kissed me on the cheek before setting me back down. Then Arianna wrapped her arms around my neck and held me while I hugged her close.

She was already crying, wetting my shirt. I didn't recall her mother being so emotional, and her father was the devil, so I didn't know where she had gotten that trait from. Either way, it made me feel good. "Hi, baby. How are you doing?"

I tried to sit down, but she continued to hold onto me. "Mom, I have missed you so much. I can't wait until you come home so I can see you every day." She kissed me on the cheek again and then sat down beside me.

The visiting room was empty for the most part, with the exception of two other families. The guards looked sleepy and a bit irritated, as if they couldn't wait until the day was over already. They were reading newspapers or dozing off in their chairs. That made me giggle.

Roman kissed me on the forehead before sitting across from me. "I been meaning to write you, but you already know how fast that world be spinning. But, on some real shit, I been missing you, boo, so I had to come on out and see you. And you already know Arianna wasn't about to let me come alone. Alexis staying with me now, too."

I was nodding my head at the first part, but at the revelation of the last part, I felt my heart skip a beat. I didn't think I heard him right. "What did you just say about Alexis?" I asked, turning my ear toward him as if that was going to make me hear him better. I wanted to make sure I got it right this time.

"You heard me. I said my little cousin now stays with me, and she has been for a few weeks now. There was a whole lot of bullshit going on at that foster home she was in, and they exposed that crap. They recorded the lady doing some ill-advised things with a couple of the kids on seven separate occasions. Her friend even set up a website that filmed some of it in real time."

I perked up. "They didn't hurt my baby, did they?"

He picked some lint off his pants and popped it to the floor, then fixed his cuff so it fit back over his Gucci shoes that matched his top. "Nall, li'l momma good. Had something happened to her, you already know that shit would have been on the World News already because I would have blown Chicago off the map. I mean that shit."

I looked around the small visiting room, confused. "I don't get it then, where is she? Why didn't she come with you guys?" I was feeling sort of hurt. I mean, if she was no longer with the Taylors what stopped her from coming to see me along with her cousin and sister?

Roman lowered his head and ran his hand over it. "Well, she ain't here."

Arianna jumped in. "But in her defense, mom, she didn't even know we were coming out to see you. It was kind of a spur of the moment thing. I just had to see you today, and Roman had given her permission to chill with her friend already."

He shook his head. "I don't know, but li'l homey seemed

cool. Rolling a BMW and all that. He looked like he had it together, and Alexis gave me that look that said she wasn't about to take no for an answer, so I folded. You know she too pretty to be saying no to, anyway."

I wasn't trying to hear none of that shit. I was still trying to wonder why she had not begged him to see me like Arianna obviously had. That made me think my daughter didn't love me, and before I could stop them, tears started coming down my cheeks. I felt like I was on the verge of breaking down. Arianna got up and came over to comfort me.

"Mom, what is the matter? Why are you crying? We thought you would be happy to see us," she whimpered, on the verge of crying along with me.

I shook my head. "No, it's not that. I just don't understand why my daughter hates me so much. Why is she not here? Don't she want to see me as much as I want to see her?"

Roman reached across the table and grabbed my hand. "Man, shorty, you tripping. Of course that girl wants to see you. Like I said, we didn't tell her we were coming. We decided this last minute, just jumped in the truck and smashed out. She had already left with her friend. But ever since she got to my house, all she has been talking about is coming out to see you. Every other topic is about you, Tiny, so you have to stop wallowing in pity because you have no reason to feel that way. She loves you, and so do we"

"Yeah, Mom, we love you to death, and you mean everything to all of us, but especially Alexis. She actually hates me because I love you so much."

"Yeah, and she told me she don't want to share you with nobody, so does that sound like a daughter that hates her mother?"

I shook my head, though I was still feeling somewhat down. I just wanted to be with her already. "Well, that's good, because I'm coming home."

Chapter 17

Alexis

Prince kept his word and bought another car twenty minutes after the old man put a dent in his hood with his cane. He bought a Mercedes AMG fresh off the lot. One minute he was getting out of his driver's seat to the car we were sitting in, and the next thing I knew he was rolling up to the car in the black-on-black Benz with all-red leather interior.

"Get out and jump in this one, ma. Fuck that car," he said, getting out and popping the trunk to the old one, taking out two suitcases and placing them into the trunk of the new car. He also went under the seat and put two firearms onto his waist. I was caught up in that thug shit, and I couldn't lie, how he was carrying on was turning me on in the worst way. He acted like a straight boss, and that was alluring to me. I liked that a whole lot. I had still not given him my flower, but if he kept at it like he was, it wouldn't be too long before I did.

He handed the keys to the older white man who got behind the wheel. At the same time Prince did a u-ey, and stormed out of the parking lot, nearly hitting a man driving a moped. He slammed on the brakes and I hit my head on the dashboard. It wasn't hard enough to do any damage, but I was still mad, just the same.

"Baby, please be careful. Damn, who are you trying to impress, anyway? I thought I was already sitting beside you," I said, rubbing my forehead and flipping down my sun visor to look into the mirror. I didn't see any scars or blood, so I just chalked that shit up as me being in a relationship with a crazed lunatic.

"Damn, shorty, my bad. But you already knew I was gon' have to try these pipes out."

He stormed out into the busy street and flew past the lights. I looked at his digital dashboard, and he was already going 101 miles an hour, weaving in and around other cars on the street. Twice he almost hit a pedestrian, and twice I almost peed in my panties. This dude was crazy, and he did not need to be behind the wheel of a fast-paced car like he was.

"Prince, you gon' kill somebody, I swear to god. And when you do, I'm dumping your ass. I'm not about to be waiting on a crazy-ass nigga that run people down with his cars just because he can. Now, I thought you was more of a boss than that."

That must have bruised his ego because he slowed down as he entered onto the expressway. "Damn, that's how you feel, though?" he asked, looking at me like he was hurt.

I was over the whole stunt boy routine. After I saw a lady had to damn near break her neck to get her child out of the street, I was seriously done with it all. It was time he acted like an adult. "Yeah, I'm saying we're supposed to be going to take care of some real business. And here you are with god only knows what in the trunk of your car, yet you're speeding and acting like an idiot. That shit is not cool, and I am not impressed. So, if that was your aim, mission failed." I rolled my eyes and looked out my window, ignoring him.

Even though I wasn't paying him no mind, I could tell he was constantly looking at me again and again, even though he wasn't saying anything. I was a little irritated, and I was silently asking myself what the hell I was getting into. Here he was talking about probably going to have to commit murder because of some foul business dealings, but all I had seen him do was act completely immature. What type of killer acted like a child? I was wondering if he knew the severity of what he was talking about doing, because I did, and I was starting to have second thoughts.

I let down my window a little further so the air could hit my face better. I closed my eyes and tried to visualize my mother's face. I took a deep breath and summoned her spirit that I knew had to be deep within me. I missed her, and for some reason I felt her missing me. I was on the verge of telling him to take me home when I opened my eyes and saw we were already way out by farms and stuff. The city of Chicago was long gone somewhere in our rearview mirrors. I felt I had missed my opportunity to escape the situation I didn't feel so good about any longer. I shook my head and closed my eyes again, praying it would all turn out for the best.

I must have been way more tired than I'd known, because I dozed off and was awakened when I heard Prince talking to a lady at the In-and-Out Burger's drive-through intercom. Coincidentally, I'd awakened at the portion where she was giving him his total. My stomach was growling, and I hoped he had ordered me something.

He paid her and we pulled around to the next window. "Damn, it's about time you woke up. I had to turn the music up a li'l bit because you were snoring and shit. But it was cute, though. I ain't gon' tell nobody." He smiled, and I almost melted all over again.

It was pitch black outside, and I could tell we were a long way from home. I looked at his gas gauge and saw it was damn near on empty, whereas before it was a full tank. I started to wonder where the hell we were. "Uh, Prince? Where the hell are we, and how long have you been driving for?"

Some heavyset black chick with a faint mustache reached out of the restaurant window and handed him a big bag of food and two pops. He got them and handed them to me, and I sat everything down and put the pops in the cup holders. She handed him a bunch of napkins, and I started looking through the bags because no matter what, I was about to at least eat a few fries. My stomach sounded like an angry canine that was ready to attack.

He pulled away from the window and we got back onto the highway.

"So, are you going to answer my question?" I asked with a mouthful of fries. Yeah, I was being rude, but damn them jokers were appealing to my taste buds. I was smacking a little bit and everything.

He looked over at me and laughed. "I see somebody hungry, huh? I should have woken you up about two hours ago, but you were lookin' so good sleeping that I didn't want to mess with you."

Two hours ago? Now I was really starting to wonder where the hell we were. I was trying to recall if he had told me before, but I couldn't. "Prince, where are we right now?"

I felt the car speed up as we got back onto the main highway. There were all kinds of big semi-trucks in each lane, and this fool was trying to drive around them like he had lost his mind or something.

"Right now, we're about thirty minutes away from Detroit. I'm about to go up here real quick and take care of some business, then we gon' get a hotel and chill for the night. I'm just hoping that all goes as planned."

I did not like hearing that uncertainty in his voice. I wanted to know what he meant about hoping things went as planned. What kind of a plan was that? "Prince, can you explain what you're talking about when you say you hope things go as planned? What are we walking into right now?" I was getting real worried, especially now that I knew we were headed to broke-down-ass Detroit. That city was way worse than Chicago to me, and them niggas out there were grimy by all means. They didn't have no remorse. I did not feel secure being with him way out there and conducting whatever business he was talking about.

He shrugged his shoulders like he had everything under control. "Nall, I'm just saying you can never be too sure about anything in this business. These niggaz could be waiting to body me. I can never be too sure. Or things can go smooth. I can make this drop off, and touch bases with dude, and we can be up and out of there as planned."

Yeah, I wasn't feeling that explanation at all. This dude was tripping. I was about to ask him to just let me out and I'd hitchhike my way back home because I was not feeling what he was putting down. I was too young to be getting killed because I was following behind a pretty boy I thought I loved. Hell nall. Things were starting to make sense, and I was ready to call it quits.

"Shorty, I'm saying you acting all scared and shit now. What's good?" He turned down his radio and kept looking from the road back to me.

I chewed up another French fry and swallowed it, then sipped from the straw in my pop. It must have gone down the wrong pipe, because I started choking for a few seconds. He reached over and patted me on the back. I still don't know why people do that, because it don't help none. After a little while I stopped coughing and thanked him for hitting me on my back anyway.

"Okay, Prince, I ain't gon' lie to you, I am scared. And the reason is because you don't even seem like you have a damn plan. You're making it seem like you're just winging it, and that's not cool with me because there are two lives at stake here, not just one. I don't know what I'm getting into, and to be honest, I think I might be having second thoughts."

He bit into his bottom lip as he drove his car with one arm, the other one hung somewhat out the window. He was silent for a long time. "Yo, keep shit hot with me. You don't think I got shit under control, do you? You think I'm just some studio gangster that's out here faking the funk, huh?" He sounded as if he were getting irritated.

At this point I was ready to speak my mind and I didn't care what happened after that. Clearly, he wanted to hear the truth and even though I knew he couldn't handle it I was still going to give it to him.

"On some real stuff, yeah, I believe all of that. I think you faking even though you don't have to. I mean, who are you trying to impress? You already have all the money. All the clothes and cars. Jewelry if you want it. That's the American dream. Why are you trying to impress people that can't even imagine having half of what you do? Sooner or later you're going to have to get it. You're going to have to understand it is more to life than materialism. On some real stuff, though, can't you see that?"

He scrunched up his face, then grunted. "Man, shorty, you can't even front like that ain't one of the reasons you started jocking me. All it took was for me to put a bundle of money on my lap, and yo' ass was all in like poker chips."

By this time, I was working one of them burgers out of the bag. I was listening to him, but I was also listening to my stomach, too, so why not kill two birds with one stone? By the time he finished with what he was saying, I had a mouthful of food and chewed with my eyes closed. I stuffed some fries in there along with the burger, and man, my mouth was in Heaven.

When he stopped talking, I sipped from my pop to wash it all down, and then I wiped my mouth and nodded at him. "Yeah, you're right, but it was way before the bundle of money. It was back when you pulled up in a foreign car and got out looking as good as you did. But the illusion of wealth definitely intrigued me, and what of it? All I'm saying is we can move past that now and get on some grown people shit. You're the one saying we're on a mission right now that could potentially bring murder, and I'm saying you absolutely must have things mapped out accordingly or we're in trouble. By the sounds of things, it feels like you're winging it, and I don't think I can get down with that. Damn, don't I have the right to feel safe? I mean, it's like I said before though: I think you're out here doing too much. What type of nigga that's riding around like you're riding and seeing the kind of money you are is still in the streets? I feel like you're just doing shit to impress others."

He frowned up his face and kept rolling without saying a word. I offered him some of the food and he simply grunted, so I shrugged my shoulders and kept on eating. I wasn't about to let his attitude ruin my meal that he had paid for. It is what it is, that's what I was feeling.

***

Sometime later that night, we pulled up in Detroit, and I felt the shivers go all through me. I just had a bad feeling about everything. Nothing seemed right, and my stomach started doing somersaults – especially when he drove through an okay-looking neighborhood of houses with lawns that were mown, then took a few back roads and wound up in a part of town so gritty it looked like people went there just to die. All the houses were boarded up, but that didn't stop people from sitting on the porches and passing bottles of alcohol back and forth. Some were smoking the pipe, and there were still others that shot needles into their veins. It seemed like there were gang bangers on every corner and in the middle of every block in big groups.

The streetwalkers looked half dead, like if you touched

them, they were guaranteed to burn you with something. The scowls on their faces were of women who had seen it all and were almost ready for it all to be over. They looked defeated and run down. They stood a safe distance from each other on their posts as if respect was an unwritten rule. To them, it seemed there was no room for an outsider.

I couldn't believe how many stray dogs we saw foaming at the mouth. Their eyes were deranged, and a few of them chased after our car. The rats that scurried on the side of the curb looked as big as cats. They put our city rats to shame, and even a few of them foamed at the mouth. I felt a chill go through me, and I wanted out of that city.

The farther we got into this neighborhood, the more fearful I became. When Prince turned into an alley that had to have more than twenty dudes in it, I thought I would pass the hell out. I thought he had lost his damn mind.

They all looked to be armed with masks on. I felt like we had driven into an ISIS safe haven.

I was so scared that I reached over and clung to his arm. "Baby, what the fuck are we doing here? Do you know these dudes?" I asked, trying not to scream because I was becoming hysterical.

"Yeah, just chill. I have to make a drop off here, and then we gon' be on our way. Don't be acting all nervous and shit, because these niggaz ain't got it all. They probably about to come and frisk you, but just roll with it. It's standard."

Standard? What the hell was he talking about? And what had he drug me into? I was shaking so bad it looked like he had locked me out in the cold.

Prince started to get out of his car, and one of the masked men pointed an assault rifle directly at his side of the car while another one smacked the hood and did the sign for him to stay in, but roll down his window. Another one of them, also in a white ski mask, stood on the side of my window and pointed two guns directly at me. The guns had clips so long they looked like table legs. The masked person had them turned sideways for dramatic effect, and best believe it was exactly how I was about to start acting: dramatic as hell because I was spooked.

Prince lowered his window, and the nose of the big rifle slid through the window and poked him in the chest. "Say, Prince, who is that bitch you got with you? I thought we said from now on we were doing business one-on-one?" He snarled, hawked, and spit a big-ass green loogie onto Prince's windshield. I almost threw up and couldn't help dry heaving.

"Yo, chill, Drill. Man, that's just my girl, dawg. We about to head west after this, and she don't know what's really good. We straight, Joe. Trust me."

Drill started laughing. "Trust you, nigga? I don't trust no muthafucka on this earth, not even my newborn baby. I feel like you're disrespecting me by asking me some shit like that, so check yourself. Now, pop the trunk and don't move, or else I'm about to body your bitch."

He snapped his fingers and about ten red dots came across my face from his men's weapons. If I thought I was losing it before, I fainted twice and woke back up before my chin hit my chest. I was so scared I was low-key passing gas.

Prince popped the trunk, and I could feel the car moving behind me. I took that as a sign the men had to retrieve whatever Prince had brought them. Meanwhile, I had these dots on my face, and I had the feeling I was about to be murdered any second. I started saying a silent prayer and wishing my mom were there. I needed her so bad. What the hell had I been thinking, following behind this fool? He had me all the way in Detroit at gunpoint. What type of shit was that?

Drill nodded his head. "So, tell me something. Is it all good?" he asked the men behind us. I couldn't hear their responses, but due to the fact he lowered his big gun and the beams turned off me, I took that as a good sign.

He reached into the window and patted Prince on the shoulder. "Well, you came through again. That's what's up. You just better hope Chris don't find out or yo' ass gon' be grass, you feel me?"

Prince pushed the assault rifle out of his face. "Man, fuck Chris. That nigga run under my father, and not the other way around. I don't owe his bitch-ass shit. Anytime I want to flood y'all out here, I'm gon' be en route. That's just how that's gon' work, point blank." He reached into the ashtray and lit up half a blunt while Drill dropped a black bag into the back seat.

"That's all there, li'l homey. It's good. Yo, before you go, though, I wanted to run something by you."

Damn, I was ready to get the fuck out of there. Why was they going through this talking routine? Wasn't business supposed to be business, and after it was concluded everybody went their own separate ways? I was getting a bad feeling being there. I wanted out.

Prince blew the smoke up toward the ceiling, causing it to float in all directions of the car. I lowered my window. I wasn't trying to catch no contact from that crap. I was already paranoid enough. I was praying this would all be over in a matter of seconds.

"Oh, yeah? Well, what's that?" he asked, leaning into the window, more intrigued.

Drill leaned all the way into the window, took the blunt from him, and pulled off of it. He blew the smoke right at me, and I fanned it away. "You sure shorty right there straight?" he asked, looking me over.

Prince waved me off. "Yeah, I told you, she don't know

what's good. She just along for the ride."

I felt so offended by his comment that I wanted to bust him in the mouth like I was a man or something. He made me feel cheap and stupid. I was hoping he was doing it in a ploy to protect me and he didn't actually feel that way. I mean, because it was obvious what his business was with those guys. We had just done some kind of a drug deal, and clearly Drill had paid him with the bag of what had to be money that he dropped on the back seat.

"A'ight, cool then. Look, my people been thinking it's about time to get rid of that nigga Chris because he is becoming too much of a headache. We thinking about bodying that nigga the next time he come out here, but if we do that, we think we might lose that plug down south, and that can't happen. Now, I know you doing your thing, too, and you got access to everything he supplies. What if we X that nigga and mainline all of our product and amphetamines straight through you? That would bump all of our wages up by 33 percent, and it would also give us the chance to spread out of Detroit toward Flint, and even down to Cleveland. I got some hotheads down there that's looking to get connected, and I'm thinking we can sew some shit up, but the first thing we have to do is body that overbearing Chris nigga."

I felt an eerie chill go through me. Call it woman's intuition or whatever, but I just felt like something wasn't right. We needed to get the hell out of there, and I was praying to God it happened soon. I kept glancing out of the window and noted how the masked men seemed as if they were getting closer to our car. Yeah, something definitely wasn't right. I wished I had been behind the wheel, because I would have peeled out a long time ago.

"So, I'm saying, Prince, what you thinking?" Drill asked, pointing his rifle upward along his shoulder. I remember thinking he reminded me of somebody from Al-Qaeda. His eyes were sinister, and it looked as if they were empty and without a soul.

Prince rubbed his chin and thought over what Drill was saying. He acted as if he was far away and in deep thought. When he started to nod his head, I got even more nervous. "On some real shit, Drill, if it was up to me, I'd body that nigga in cold blood and leave it at that. I ain't never got along with big homey. I always felt like he ain't like me because of who I was or something, so it's always been 'fuck him' in my heart. But, that's my man's pops, and I wouldn't want to hurt him like that. If it was up to me, and he ain't have no connections to him, then I'd personally body that nigga. That's on everything I love, too." He slammed his fist onto his chest over his heart.

Drill shook his head. "Yeah, but business is supposed to be business. Sometimes in business you have to trim the fat, and right now that nigga is obese to us. Something gotta be done about it. I'm trying to get to seeing numbers, and homey is standing in the way of that. He be shitting on us out here in the SIX, and that shit can't keep happening. Now, I thought I would bring this to your attention because you seem like you're in the process of becoming a shrewd businessman, but it seems like you ain't got no balls, though."

Prince bit into his bottom lip and adjusted himself in his seat. "Oh, nigga, I got balls. It's just I was trying to factor in my mans, and –"

"And fuck all them emotions, nigga. It's either you're with us or you ain't. Now, word is out your Pops beefing heavy with them Jamaicans. They say they got dread-heads coming all the way from the island to put metal to that nigga. I got killas on deck to roll out, and even hop on a plane if need be to cut them dread-heads off at the neck. We all willing to put in work, but in order for me to weave my army into that of your old man's, we gotta get our bands up. And in order to do that, Chris gotta get bodied. So I'm saying, what's it gon' be? I know you ain't saying your guy's pop's life is worth more than your own."

Damn, I wanted to get the fuck out of there. Now these dudes were talking about mass killings and traveling to commit murder. I was starting to feel sick to my stomach. How could Prince even think about killing Li'l Chris's father? He was, after all, his right-hand man, and the same went for his father and Chris. They had grown up together, and as one they had taken over Chicago in a bloody way. I didn't like where this was headed, and I wished I wasn't there to hear it.

Prince looked as uncomfortable as I was. All he kept on doing was fidgeting in his seat. "Yo, you know what? that shit ain't got nothing to do with me, Drill. If you want to body that nigga, then fuck him. Do you. Ain't no blood on my hands, and life goes on."

Drill gave him an evil grin. "That shit sound slick, but I still need you to give that order, and I need to know once we body this nigga, you gon' plug directly into us out here and help us to expand our operations. All I need is the nod, and we can shake on this shit."

Prince looked as if he was just ready to get out of there. He nodded his head and then shook Drill's hand.

That's when Drill took a step back and pointed his assault rifle directly at Prince's forehead. "Scoot over, nigga, I'm about to take you somewhere to cement this shit in stone. After you take care of this little business, you can be on your way."

***

I had tears rolling down my cheeks. Why the hell were we

rolling down a long sewage tunnel on ORVs? And why did the dude sitting behind me on my four-wheeler have a gun pressed to the back of my head? To my right I could smell the waste of the city as it flowed in the muddy and bile-infested water alongside of us. It was pitch black all around, with the exception of the lights coming from the five four-wheelers. In front of me Drill sat behind Prince with his rifle pressed to his neck. The roar of our vehicles were the only sounds of the night.

We pulled into a big, concrete-looking thing that was in the shape of a circle. It had more than a hundred cat-sized rats running through its waters, and they tried to escape in every directly as we drove directly at them and into the tunnel.

Once again, blackness surrounded me, and the stench of death was so strong I could not breathe. The air felt thick, and I felt trapped. We followed the brake lights of the vehicle in front of us until we entered another tunnel that led to more water splashing, and when some got into my mouth, I threw up a little. The smell in there was the worst I have ever experienced in my life.

We came out on the other end of a small river that led to a huge warehouse. In front of the warehouse were a bunch of black-on-black trucks and Ducatis. We were made to park our vehicles, and the man behind me wrapped his fingers into my hair and forced me inside the building. We took three flights of stairs through darkness until we got to the third floor, where we were met by light and a group of men with all-black masks. Me and Prince were forced to the center of the group, and there we were forcibly made to sit down in chairs.

Drill walked to the front of the room and stood behind a man in a white mask. They whispered to each other before the man gave him half a hug and proceeded to walk up to us. I was so scared I almost fainted. I was shaking in my heels. In fact, I had lost one of my heels and my toes were covered in sewage. I had something crawling on my feet that I was trying hard not to pay attention to, and something else was crawling up my leg.

The man walked over to Prince and slapped him so hard his chair fell backward. I could hear him moaning to the side of me, and then his char was sat back into place. The man swung again and knocked him back out of his seat. This time I could not hear him making a sound. He came over and knelt before me. I closed my eyes because I knew my ass-whoopin' was next, and if he had flipped Prince over with one hit, then my li'l black ass was out.

I was surprised when the blows didn't come. Instead, he lifted his mask from his face and smiled at me. "So, you're Alexis, huh?"

How did he know my name? What was going on? Why was he looking at me like he knew something I did not know? Was he going to kill me? What had I gotten myself into? I don't know where I got the strength or the gall to ask him the question, but I had to know. "Who are you? And how do you know my name?"

He gave me an evil smile, then he leaned forward and kissed me on the lips. "Well, my name is Jaheim. Me and your mother are old friends, and she owes me a lot of money. And you're going to help me get it from her." He looked down at Prince, who was still knocked out. "And he has a role in all of this as well. Ain't that right, family?"

I looked all around the room as more and more men started to pile into the big warehouse until it was so packed they could not move without bumping into somebody. There was a lot of murmuring going on until Jaheim held up his hand in the sky, then all was silent. When he dropped it, all the masked men shed their masks, and out dropped their long, flowing dreadlocks.

"This is the beginning of a new dawn." He walked over to me and rubbed my chin. "You belong to me, Alexis. You're my princess, and I got plans for you."

All I could do was swallow.

Chapter 18

Tiny

I had one more day until I was out of this dump and finally back out in the free world. I could not wait. It seemed like the day was moving at a snail's pace, and it was driving me crazy. I could not sit still. Every time I tried to compose myself, I started to think about going home and being able to be with my daughter for the first time, and it made my eyes water. I was so worried about her. It was my intention to call Roman's phone before they ended our day space-time, but I didn't get the chance because I was filling out paperwork.

In my cell, I lay back on my bed with my eyes closed. I was trying to get some type of rest because my mind was going a hundred miles an hour, and it had been that way ever since I'd found out I was leaving a week ago. No matter what I did, sleep would not find me.

Deena jumped down off her bunk and knelt at my feet. "I'm going to miss you, baby." She sounded like she was ready to cry again, and I was hoping she wouldn't because I was all cried out. I was over the whole prison scene, and I wanted to be out of there. I had done everything she'd wanted to do the last six days, sexually. Now I just wanted to be alone, and I could tell she sensed it because five minutes later, after I had not responded to her caresses, she jumped back into her bed and I could hear her crying again.

I don't know what took place inside the rec yard, but that night I neglected to attend recreation, and for some reason every guard in the prison rushed out to the rec field while the rest of the prison was shut down. Deena lay sleeping away in her bed, oblivious to the fact. Having cried for two hours straight with no response from me had put her out like a light.

***

The next morning did not come soon enough. I tossed and turned in my bed, and finally an hour before the sun came up I drifted off to sleep, only to be awakened by one of the guards banging on my door. I shot up like the place was on fire.

"Inmate #E353677, pack your things. It's time to go!"

I walked out of the prison doors toward the gate that had held me captive for nearly 18 years. I could not believe I was actually walking out of them, and I couldn't stop the tears from falling as I got closer and closer to the release site.

I could see Roman and all the girls waiting for me in the parking lot. I made out Arianna. I couldn't quite make out through the distance which one was Alexis, but I could not wait to see my baby.

Finally, I quit all the formalities and started to jog directly toward the guards in front of my release point. Once there, they nodded and opened the gates. I stepped through and Arianna rushed me right away and wrapped her arms around me.

"Mommy, they have Alexis, and they aren't letting her go. They say we owe them for the pains of the past, and I have no idea what that means."

I could barely make out everything she was saying because she was crying at the same time. Her friends came up and hugged me with tears in their eyes. Roman was the last. He stood in front of me and handed me an envelope. I looked into his eyes, and he avoided mine.

I took the envelope from him. It had already been opened, so I took out its contents. It read:

Welcome home, Zivial. We have a lot of unfinished

business. You owe me, an eye for an eye. Alexis being returned to you comes with a price. I'll be in touch. Oh, and it's true what they say. Chocolate does melt in your mouth.

Signed,
an old friend

Before I could fully process what I had read and what it meant, my knees hit the concrete and I broke down crying.

They had taken my baby all because of me. I had failed her once again, and now I didn't know what to do. One thing I did know was I was willing to do anything for her, no matter the costs.

And before it was all said and done, I would.

To Be Continued…
Loyal to the Game 3
Coming Soon

Stay Connected with Us!

Text **LOCKDOWN** to 22828 to stay up-to-date with new releases, sneak peaks, contests and more…

Thank you!

By **Eddie "Wolf" Lee**

A HUSTLER'S DECEIT **II**

THE BOSS MAN'S DAUGHTERS **III**

BAE BELONGS TO ME **II**

By **Aryanna**

A KINGPIN'S AMBITON

By **Ambitious**

Available Now

(CLICK TO PURCHASE)

RESTRAINING ORDER **I & II**

By **CA$H & Coffee**

LOVE KNOWS NO BOUNDARIES **I II & III**

By **Coffee**

LAY IT DOWN **I & II**

LAST OF A DYING BREED

By **Jamaica**

LOYAL TO THE GAME

By **TJ & Jelissa**

PUSH IT TO THE LIMIT

By **Bre' Hayes**

BLOOD OF A BOSS **I II & III**

By **Askari**

THE STREETS BLEED MURDER **I, II & III**

THE HEART OF A GANGSTA

By **Jerry Jackson**

CUM FOR ME

CUM FOR ME 2

CUM FOR ME 3

An **LDP Erotica Collaboration**

BRIDE OF A HUSTLA **I & II**

By **Destiny Skai**

WHEN A GOOD GIRL GOES BAD

By **Adrienne**

A GANGSTER'S REVENGE **I II III & IV**

THE BOSS MAN'S DAUGHTERS

THE BOSS MAN'S DAUGHTERS II

A SAVAGE LOVE **I & II**

BAE BELONGS TO ME

By **Aryanna**

A DOPEBOY'S PRAYER

By **Eddie "Wolf" Lee**

WHAT ABOUT US **I & II**

NEVER LOVE AGAIN

THUG ADDICTION

By **Kim Kaye**

THE KING CARTEL **I, II & III**

By **Frank Gresham**

THESE NIGGAS AIN'T LOYAL **I, II & III**

By **Nikki Tee**

GANGSTA SHYT **I II &III**

By **CATO**

THE ULTIMATE BETRAYAL

By **Phoenix**

DON'T FU#K WITH MY HEART **I & II**

By **Linnea**

BOSS'N UP **I & II**

By **Royal Nicole**

I LOVE YOU TO DEATH

By Destiny J

I RIDE FOR MY HITTA

I STILL RIDE FOR MY HITTA

By **Misty Holt**

LOVE & CHASIN' PAPER

By **Qay Crockett**

TO DIE IN VAIN

Loyal to the Game 2

By **ASAD**

BOOKS BY LDP'S CEO, CA$H
(CLICK TO PURCHASE)

TRUST IN NO MAN

TRUST IN NO MAN 2

TRUST IN NO MAN 3

BONDED BY BLOOD

SHORTY GOT A THUG

THUGS CRY

THUGS CRY 2

THUGS CRY 3

TRUST NO BITCH

TRUST NO BITCH 2

TRUST NO BITCH 3

TIL MY CASKET DROPS

RESTRAINING ORDER

RESTRAINING ORDER 2

IN LOVE WITH A CONVICT

Coming Soon

BONDED BY BLOOD 2

BOW DOWN TO MY GANGSTA

www.ingramcontent.com/pod-product-compliance
Lightning Source LLC
Chambersburg PA
CBHW070016260626
47159CB00005B/1837